A Word to the Wise About
THE BIG FRAME

THERE have been many mystery novels about the "fourth estate," but this is the first in many moons with a great syndicated Sunday newspaper supplement as a background, such as the famous *American Weekly* and *This Week*, those multi-million circulation feature sections distributed through scores of newspapers all over America.

THE BIG FRAME is concerned with *Phalanx*, newly spawned syndicate of the multi-million dollar Rideout interests, its editors, writers, camera men, etc., whose own personal ambitions, greed, hates and jealousies f o m e n t enough dynamite to blow the front page off any paper in the country!

Here is authentic color, action and rapid-fire writing that will keep you entertained to the "nth" degree from beginning to end!

The

BIG FRAME

▼▼▼▼▼▼▼▼▼▼▼▼▼▼▼▼▼▼▼▼▼▼▼▼▼▼▼▼▼▼▼▼

▲▲▲▲▲▲▲▲▲▲▲▲▲▲▲▲▲▲▲▲▲▲▲▲▲▲▲▲▲▲▲▲

A MYSTERY NOVEL BY

Sam Merwin, Jr.

WILDSIDE PRESS

ONE

TONY YOUNG TILTED far back in the pseudo-mahogany swivel chair behind his green-blottered desk and watched Paul Stanton light a cigar. Paul always made a sacred ceremony of it — he held it well away from his mouth, turned it in a slow circle over the match until the flame caught evenly.

"Phalanx is in," said Paul after a quartet of preliminary puffs. "We're going to be the biggest thing to hit the Sunday supplement field since the *American Weekly* turned into a gold mine for Hearst. This last trip of mine is going to do the same job for young Hank Rideout."

"So you really think we can do it," Tony said.

He looked out the window beside his desk at a narrow vista of midtown Manhattan. He ran the New York office for Phalanx, newly spawned newspaper syndicate for the Rideout interests, whose headquarters were in Philadelphia, where the parent paper flourished. The founding of the Sunday supplement was the primary step in getting the syndicate on its feet.

"I know damned well we can," said Paul, crossing his well pressed legs to reveal a stretch of pearl-gray spat. "You know how the war has hit everything. Well, war or no war, I've signed up Sunday papers in Cleveland, Detroit and St. Louis. And in less than three weeks, mind you. With what we've got now — Boston, Atlanta, Chicago, and the parent sheet in Philly — this gives us as solid a setup for syndication as any Sunday magazine in the country. You realize what the success of Phalanx will mean to you, Tony?"

Tony nodded, lit a cigarette. He liked to hear Paul talk. When it came to his chosen business, Stanton was clear, concise and sure of himself. He'd certainly shown himself to be a monster salesman. The younger man found it close to incredible.

"It means," Paul went on, "that you'll get three hundred a week minimum for just sitting behind that desk of yours here in New York while we get the book out in Philly. Which is twice what you're getting now. And as Phalanx grows, so will your salary and opportunity."

"What," said Tony quietly, "about Malin Pierce? He may have been a titan twenty years ago for Holloway Johnson, but he's a clinker in the grate of progress today. In the six months I've been here, I've averaged ten story ideas a week out of this office — all but a half dozen of them ahead of the other supplements.

"So what happens?" Tony went on, his voice lifting a trifle. He got angry whenever he let his thoughts range to the obese monstrosity, Malin Pierce, who was his immediate editorial superior. "By the time Pierce gets around to printing any of these yarns I feed him, they're ancient history. With him in charge, it's a miracle the magazine gets out at all."

Stanton, for once, said nothing. He nodded gravely, revealing thin, carefully brushed light hair across his pink pate each time his head bobbed.

Tony lit a cigarette and let his vision of grotesque

Malin Pierce fade before a shining grail of amber ale with a collar on it. He'd been up most of the night chasing an angle on a story of taxi dancers clipping service men on leave and had, purely in the course of duty, absorbed an overdose of handout Scotch. Paul looked healthy and thoroughly kempt in comparison to the way Tony felt.

"You're doing all right, kid," said Paul. He patted the hair even smoother over the top of his thinning head with a practiced gesture, and got to his feet. "We've simply got to work around and in spite of Pierce until we can muscle him out of the job. It's not going to be easy — old M. P. has connections with Hank Rideout that date way back. But we've still got to get him out of here. Too many other jobs — and I'm including yours and mine — depend on making this thing go. Maybe he was a hot chimney ten years ago, but he's dangling on the ropes now. So get even more stories — we're going to need them."

"I'll do my damnedest, Paul," said Tony. He pulled an assignment sheet from the top drawer of his desk. "I've got twenty-two items here for immediate or imminent local attention. And I've got Miss Rankin clipping every local paper and mag to pieces. She's got eyes like a well bred hawk."

"I didn't look at her eyes," said Paul. "She has too many other notable items." He licked a corner of his lips and made an hourglass with facile hands. "What's her first name?"

"Lee," said Tony. "And job or no job, if I find you mucking around her, Paul, I'll wring your scrawny neck."

"Hello!" said Paul. "I thought you had enough woman trouble without taking on more. Well, it's nice trouble."

"That's what you think," said Tony.

"You're a lucky stiff having that bum knee."

"If you're implying I'm a draft dodger," said Tony, getting hot, "don't tell me you haven't got some angle doped out for keeping out of uniform. You're not so old."

"Thanks for the kind words," said Paul, preening himself and tugging at his lapels. He looked vaguely like a bantam cock. "No, I wasn't figuring on the military angle, Tony. You're one of the few ex-football heroes who doesn't have to be a moron to appeal to the gals' maternal instincts. Just a few twinges on a damp day will bring them flocking around with hot compresses — and I mean hot."

"Get out, louse," said Tony, laughing.

Paul put on his Anthony Eden, gave it a rap with his fingers and lifted a hand in salute.

"I'll do that very thing," he said. "I've got to catch the eleven o'clock for Philly and give young Rideout my report. So long."

Tony walked to the door of the office with Paul, watched him narrowly as he moved past the monitor board at which Lee Rankin sat buffing her nails. Paul paused, winked deliberately, and departed.

It was impossible to dislike Paul Stanton, Tony reflected as he sauntered out to get a drink of water in the lavatory. He was cheap, crude, generally impossible, half stuffed shirt, half whole-hearted lecher. But there was an unsinkable good humor that combined with alert intelligence and a cracking vitality, passed as a pretty good substitute for charm.

Wishing wistfully that it were beer, Tony downed three cupfuls of tepid water and came back to his office. When he walked in, Lee Rankin was answering the telephone, her long-bobbed dark brown head atilt as she talked down into the mouthpiece.

"No," she was saying in the honeyed tones of her telephone voice, "Mr. Young stepped out for a moment."

She stuck out her tongue at him as he took the instrument away from her. The caller was Connie Talbot, publicity woman for a wide number of metropolitan enterprises.

"Unless I'm nuts, I've got a yarn for you, Tony," Connie said.

"Give, baby," he told her. "We need them like crazy."

"I fell over it in the Hotel Van Dyke," Connie said. "I've taken over their account. They want some guests."

"That's a yarn in itself," said Tony. "I thought everybody in that mausoleum had a ninety-nine-year lease. What is it?"

"It's an agoraphobe," said Connie.

"Old stuff," Tony told her. "That professor out West has been written up a full dozen times by every Sunday supplement alive. You ought to remember that one. He got scared by a train or something and his nurse didn't change his diapers in time.

"He couldn't get out of the bathroom or something for the rest of his life. But he got married four times — that's what kept the story going."

"Of course I remember it," snapped Connie Talbot. "But this one has a couple of new slants. The gent has a daughter that's good for a couple of hot licks, and he's just about cured after living there in the Van Dyke in two rooms for twenty years."

"How does he know he's cured?" asked Tony. "If this turns out to be as phony as your last tip, babe, I'll paddle your bottom. Most of these guys are fakes."

"Doc Remsen's working on this one. He's my authority," she told him.

Tony whistled, and his eyebrows rose. Remsen was a great psychiatrist of impeccable reputation.

"Okay," he said. "I'll come over and bring Carl Martin along to take some shots if the gal's any good at all. What's her claim to fame besides holding Papa's hand?"

"She wants to go on the stage," said Connie.

"Oh, Lord!" groaned Tony. "I knew there was a smell to this. Of course I don't suppose a female left tackle named Connie Talbot has made a little deal in case she clicks. I ought to turn you down cold."

"But you won't," said Connie quickly. "She's really a honey. Room six-o-eight at the Van Dyke. The name is Regis Saunders."

"Regis!" said Tony. "That's a hell of a name for a girl."

"That's her father — the agoraphobe," said Connie. "Make it eleven on the dot if you can. And thanks."

"We'll be there," said Tony dismally.

He handed the telephone back to Lee Rankin. She had wide-set gray eyes, a full mouth that turned quietly up at the corners, perfect skin, an upper-case bosom. She wore a simple hundred-dollar suit that failed slyly to hide any of the slim curves of her body. The single strand of pearls around her neck were real, though it was impossible for a layman to tell them from the five-and-ten-cent-store variety.

"Get Carl in here," said Tony. "And tell him to load up first. We've got to pay a visit to an agoraphobe with a gorgeous daughter."

"Something tells me I should have cut that call," said Lee. "What's an agoraphobe, Tony?"

She completed her connection to the little square studio down the hall where able, irascible Carl Martin worked on his prints and negatives. Then she asked the question again. Her face was tipped up toward his, and Tony kissed her soundly on the lips.

"I thought you didn't believe in making love to your employees," she told him.

Tony ruffled her well combed hair, and she knocked his hand away with a sharp slap.

"You know your status here isn't orthodox," he said, wiping dark red lipstick from around his mouth with a handkerchief. "Besides, after the cracks Paul Stanton made about you, honey, I thought I'd better find out right quick if it was still all right."

"Was it?" she asked, round-eyed and suddenly innocent.

Tony kissed her again, again ruffled her hair. She

snapped at his wrist with her teeth, then made a face.

"The way he looked at me!" she burst out. "I could feel his eyes boring right through my back. I felt as though I were sitting here stark naked."

"That wouldn't be exactly stark," said Tony, lighting a cigarette. "But it's an idea. Here's Carl. So long, honey."

"Hey, you goon, what's an agoraphobe?" she asked again.

Carl Martin was standing in the doorway. He was almost as tall as Tony, loosely built with joint articulation generally reminiscent of one of those cardboard Halloween skeletons.

"An agoraphobe, babe," Carl said gravely, "is a jerk who's afraid to come out in the open. In other words, he can start to go somewhere, but then he bumps into an imaginary wall and has to go back. I shot one once out in Queens."

"Agoraphobia," said Tony, "is the diametric opposite of claustrophobia. But it's a lot rarer. That's why — especially with a little cheesecake to dress it up — it might be good for half a page."

"Oh," said Lee Rankin, still a bit vague. "I get the cheesecake. Stay away from it, and have a good time, boys."

They rode down in the elevator, walked into a bar around the corner on Forty-fourth Street, and downed a couple of beers apiece. As the Van Dyke was close at hand, they decided to walk it.

The hotel, situated a block south of Grand Central Station, was wholly mid-Victorian in appearance. Its seven stories, encrusted in red brick and adorned with circular balconies of wrought iron, rose benignly above lower Park Avenue. The lobby, at least twenty-five feet high, was a masterpiece of waste space and red plush, sprinkled liberally with potted palm trees. The elevators were vast open iron grilles which moved from floor to floor with rheumatic dignity.

"Hell!" Tony snapped as they left the cage on the

sixth floor. "By my watch we're ten minutes early."

"So what?" said Carl Martin listlessly. He shrugged his shoulders, stepped forward and banged on the door.

Nothing happened. He rapped again, turned to Tony.

"You sure this is the room, kid?" he asked.

"It's the room, all right," said Tony.

Martin tried the knob. The door was unlocked. Poking his head inside, the photographer stayed there, seemingly stricken with paralysis. Tony gave him a poke in the kidneys, at which Carl jumped a foot, finally pulled back and looked around.

"Take a look, kid," Carl croaked.

TONY DID A DOUBLE TAKE, then followed the photographer's suggestion. His beer came flooding into his throat, and he barely avoided being violently ill on the spot. A man's body was lying on its side in the middle of a cluttered and otherwise mustily charming old-world drawing room.

Gray hair was dappled with crimson, and the carpet had purpled a pool of blood, portions of which still reflected the bright morning sunlight that poured in through the windows. The jaw and some of the rest of the face had been shot away.

"Come on, Carl," snapped Tony, his voice perforce low as he won the fight for self-control. "Wipe that doorknob and step inside."

He walked in, closed the door with his foot behind him, and looked around the room. The weapon, an old-fashioned six-gun, was lying on the carpet close to what appeared to be the entrance to the bedrooms of the suite. About two feet away from the weapon lay a bulging black wallet from which dog-eared papers protruded en masse. There couldn't, Tony told himself incredulously, be two wallets like that in the world.

Turning almost furtively to discover whether Carl had noticed it, he saw that the cameraman was standing edgily near the body, looking, with his eyes fixed and bulging, more than a little like a hypnotist's subject.

"For Christ's sake, get some shots," said Tony. "We've really fallen into something here. We're on the scene of a murder before the police. And if Connie told the truth, she and the babe will be here in less than five minutes."

"Since when was a publicity hound ever right about anything?" muttered the photographer rhetorically. He unslung his gear hastily and went to work with the single-mindedness of the expert.

Tony took advantage of his concentration to get between his mate and the wallet, stooped to pick it up. Yes, his hunch about it had been correct. In worn stamped gold letters it bore the name *Malin Pierce*.

For a full minute, while the flash bulb flared three times in quick succession, Tony just stood there. The whole thing was incomprehensible. He was tempted to pinch himself, make sure he wasn't dreaming this. He closed his eyes, opened them again. That damning name was still on the wallet.

He made his decision then. He was anything but in love with his boss editor. Pierce was like a great whale, blundering and ruthless, threatening all sorts of lesser creatures within its range — himself included — at every slap of its flukes. But like a whale, Pierce was curiously helpless, even appealing in a grotesque way. Tony couldn't conceive of his committing a cold-blooded murder.

He stuffed the wallet into his own breast pocket, where it bulged uncomfortably with his own. Then, disregarding Carl Martin's reproachful stare, Tony pulled out a handkerchief and picked up the gun. Stooping, he put the gun in the dead man's hand.

"Put it back, kid," whispered Carl Martin hoarsely. "You'll get us both jugged for this."

"Not unless you talk," said Tony. "Now take a couple more shots just in case we get caught. Then scram back to the office quick and hide them. Get moving!"

Tony left him there hard at work, wandered into the near bedroom. The bed had already been made, and from the bureau, the silver-framed sepia photograph of a stunning blonde regarded him seriously. It was inscribed in a square, feminine hand — *To Daddy, from Janet*. He tucked it away under his coat, frame and all, went through an archaic, copper-tubbed bathroom into a larger corner chamber.

There was another already made bed in here and a desk — the latter barricaded behind a huge globe that still showed Austria-Hungary and a dictionary stand complete with Webster. The rest of the room was cluttered up with sheer nylon stockings, furbelows, a vanity cluttered with cosmetics and perfume. Evidently the blonde daughter slept in her father's work room.

He retraced his steps to the first bedroom, went to work on the top drawer in the old-fashioned cherry bureau. Inside it were a collar box, military brushes, and other masculine impediments. Opening the collar box on impulse, he found himself staring at a sheaf of documents. On the topmost was typed the name, *Curtis Lamar*.

The name rang a bell in his memory, but in his confused mental state, he was unable to associate it with its source. Underneath the papers, which he stuffed hurriedly in a side pocket, were a heavy gold watch and chain. He turned the watch over.

> *To Curtis Lamar for invaluable services to*
> *Holloway Johnson.*

The *Holloway Johnson* was written in facsimile of the late famed newspaper publisher's own well remembered handwriting. At the bottom of the case it was dated — 1916. He put it in his other side pocket, hurried back to the drawing room to see if Carl Martin had finished. He bumped into the cameraman in the bedroom doorway.

"There's somebody outside in the hall," said Martin, his voice still hoarse. "It sounds like two dames — talking. What are we going to do now, boss?"

"Get the hell out of here — I hope," said Tony. "I spotted another door in the inside bedroom. This way."

He found it, fumbled with the knob, feared for a dreadful moment that they were trapped. Then it opened, and they stepped into the corridor. As Tony closed it silently, a dreadful series of screams from the drawing room made the air around them quiver.

"Take the elevator, Carl," whispered Tony. "If anyone tries to stop you and asks what you're doing here, tell him you came up with me. No one answered our knock — get that — and I went down to kill time with Leon Satterlee in Four-twenty-eight. You got wandering around in these corridors and lost yourself. You don't know nothing from nothing."

"I've got it," said Carl. "See you in jail."

"You bury those pictures first," said Tony, and raced down the carpeted stairs three at a time.

Room 428 was at the end of a right-angled corridor on the north side of the old hotel. He paused before knocking to get his breath under control. Then, setting his teeth, he lifted the brass door knocker.

Shuffling footsteps responded, and the door was opened a scant few inches. A small, oddly birdlike head peered through the gap. Thick-lensed tortoise-shell spectacles magnified the eyes to almost double their real size, putting the entire face out of drawing, giving it the look of an unsettled owl.

"Oh!" exclaimed a precise, almost shrill voice. "It's you." The strange face grew murderous in its malevolence. "Haven't I told you at least thirty-eight times never to come here to see me without telephoning in advance first?"

"That's right," said Tony, "and you're redundant, Leon. Come on, old man, don't take it so hard. I happened to be in the neighborhood and had a couple of questions I wanted to ask you. So here I am."

The head began to bob up and down in a sort of paroxysm. Tony cupped his hands to catch those distorting spectacles if they should — as seemed imminent — fall off.

When this seizure at last subsided, Leon Satterlee pulled the door open and stood revealed — all five feet four of him—clad in an amazing Chinese silk dressing gown with gold and red and blue pagodas all over it.

"Well, since you're here, I suppose you might as well come in," said Satterlee with a jerky and feminine gesture of annoyance, "but your appalling rudeness in breaking in on me like this has been a severe shock—a very severe shock."

He led the way with quick, mincing steps along a short foyer into a living room in which virtually all usual furniture had been replaced with filing cabinets — steel files, wooden files, cardboard files — heaped one on top of the other in apparently haphazard array.

"And furthermore," he went on, turning abruptly, "it's perfectly terrible to me that a man afflicted as I am should be subject to having his privacy shattered by cheap news mongers."

He began to shake all over like a shimmy dancer. Two great tears rolled down his flaccid cheeks. Tony shook his head and smiled sadly at him.

"Steady, brother Satterlee," he said. "It's really not as bad as all that. This cheap news monger pays you a pretty fair income for your services."

"To think that I should have to rely on such people for the means of my existence!" said Satterlee, reveling in self-pity.

Tony felt like saying, "Oh, yeah?" but didn't. Satterlee had, in his prosperous years, been chief feeder for the notorious Colonel Mann and his blackmailing

Town Topics, once the terror of society.

"This matter I want to ask you about, Satterlee," he said as pleasantly as he could, "is urgent, else I shouldn't have risked putting you through this. Take it easy, will you?"

"Take it *easy!*" Satterlee almost screamed like a nerve-frayed woman. "What do you want to know?"

Satterlee's shattered nerves were an old story to Tony by this time. They were considerably more than a nuisance in dealing with the little man, but Satterlee was, in his own quaint way, invaluable to him.

Sprung from origins and name unknown, this walking mass of screaming teledendrons had been for many years a hanger-on on the outer fringes of society, a shakedown artist.

With his ultimate exposure — he'd had enough on the district attorney to keep himself out of the Tombs — Satterlee collapsed. But meanwhile he had assembled an immense amount of information regarding the great and near-great of the *haute monde,* the theater, the sporting word, and the *demi monde* in America, England and, in some cases, on the Continent.

With his nervous breakdown and generally close confinement to his hotel suite, the little man had set about adding to and cross-developing his mass of intimate knowledge until his files contained little-known facts enough to rock the entire "great world" from Hollywood to Moscow. What his purpose was now that his wings had been clipped by the law, no one knew, probably least of all himself.

Perhaps it had become a vice, something he could not stop doing. Whatever the cause, it had turned profitable. Not that he'd sell his information to many persons.

For some reason, perhaps because Tony had gone to Princeton and a preparatory school which rated high on the social list — his parents had long since died broke — Leon Satterlee had taken an unexpected and

17

rather disconcerting liking to him.

Abruptly stopping his nervous jerks, Satterlee seated himself daintily behind his littered desk.

"All right, Young," he said, his voice suddenly steady. "What is it this time?"

"Well," said Tony, deciding on a direct attack and to hell with the consequences, "I want to know what you know about a man named Curtis Lamar."

Prepared for come what might, the effect of this question startled Tony, even accustomed as he was to the little man's eccentricities. Satterlee burst into a fit of violent weeping, put his head down and banged it against the desk to punctuate his sobs.

"Leave me alone!" he wailed. "Leave me alone! Can't you see I'm not in any shape — that I can't talk to you now? Go away! And don't come back here — *ever!*"

Tony got to his feet in a hurry. This, he saw, wasn't going to get him anywhere. Satterlee had taken his handkerchief out and was flicking it wildly toward the door. Its white surface was blotched with blood that had not yet turned to rust.

"Cut yourself shaving!" Tony muttered to himself as he breathed once more in the corridor. "Oh, *yeah?*"

As he rode down in the elevator, the loot in his pockets felt heavy and conspicuous. The lobby was cluttered with policemen in and out of uniform. Tony looked them over and ducked out quickly.

TWO

WHEN HE WALKED into the anteroom of his office, Lee Rankin regarded him with a shadow of anxiety in her dark eyes.

"What's eating Carl?" she said. "He came in here on rubber legs and went down the hall to the developing room and locked himself in. Now you don't look so good yourself, darling."

Tony brushed right past her, in no mood for explanation. He was weak with relief at having gotten back to his office safely with the items he'd lifted from the Saunders apartment. Moving slowly, he took off his coat, hung it carelessly on the rack in the corner. He rummaged for the loot, put it on the desk. Lee, curious and not to be put off so easily, came in and found him there with it a few moments later.

She leaned over him so that one shoulder brushed his cheek, her soft brown hair falling almost into his eyes, as she looked over his head at the papers, the gold watch and, most especially, at the photograph of the blonde honey. Tony continued to say nothing.

"Is that the cheesecake?" she asked. "She looks about your speed." Then, when Tony still failed to speak, she exploded. "For Pete's sake! What goes on?"

"Sorry, Lee," he answered finally. "I'm on the ragged edge of being in a bad jam, and I want you to do something for me after we close up for the week-end. Pierce will be in on the one o'clock from Philly, and I'm going to be sewed up for lunch with him. That may take hours—you know Malin."

"But we have a date!" wailed the girl. "Tony, if you're standing me up, I'll—"

"I'm not," said Tony. "At least not by choice. The old dodo called me this morning before you got here. I'll have him out of the way by three o'clock—that's a promise, honey — and we can have the rest of the day to ourselves."

"That's great!" she said with soft but biting sarcasm. "But if you're not through by three — "

"I'll break a leg trying. And I'm serious about this jam. Carl and I walked in on a murder cold, and I stuck my neck out."

"Tony!" she said. "It's a rib."

"Sorry," he told her. "I'm not kidding. We must have just missed it, and if the police find we were there, there'll be holy hell to pay. I want you to make copies of these documents" — he pointed to the cheaf of papers on his desk — "and then I want you to go over to the library and get the *Times* Index and dig up all you can on a guy named Curtis Lamar. The date on this watch here should start you. Work both ways from it."

"So you've turned petty thief!" said the girl.

"Sure," said Tony. He managed to smile. "You should know, babe, by this time."

His smile faded, and worry again shaded his gaze at her. Suddenly relenting, Lee came close to him again and put an arm around his shoulders and pulled his head against her.

"Don't look like that, darling," she said. "It makes me ill to see you worried. We're smarter than any police." She shook her head, and her hair got in his eyes. "It's a hell of a lot of work for a Saturday afternoon, but for you I'll do it." She picked up the documents and went out.

Tony pulled out Malin Pierce's thick wallet and examined its contents. Apart from eighty-three dollars, numerous identification papers and honorary police cards from various cities and an unintelligible heap of sloppily kept notes, there appeared to be nothing there that connected the editor with the murder of Regis Saunders or Curtis Lamar or whatever the dead man's name had been.

He looked everything over carefully twice, then gave up and shoved the money and papers back into the wallet. Putting it back in his breast pocket, he rose a trifle wearily and went down the corridor to Carl's tiny studio.

"Did you get away from there clean" Tony asked through red-tinted darkness.

Carl was rubbing a print to bring it to proper sharpness in the stinking developing fluid. He looked up and nodded.

"Yeah," he said. "Nobody asked me anything. The place was in too much of a ferment. How about you?"

"Okay," said Tony. "How are the pictures?"

"Take a look."

A set of prints, fresh from the fluid, was lying limply on the drying plate. They were good, all right.

"What in hell do you want me to do with them?" Carl inquired acidly. "They're plenty hot, Tony. If any of the boys from Centre Street ever find them, we can both kiss the girls good-bye for a longer time than I like to think about."

"Better keep the negatives — bury them somewhere your own mother wouldn't think of looking," said Tony. "And you might as well destroy the prints. They don't tell us anything we don't know already."

When Tony got back to his own office, the telephone rang. It was Philadelphia, with instructions for him to meet Malin Pierce at the Madison Avenue Longchamps in half an hour. Tony promised to be there, wondered why Pierce hadn't set the date in the first place and saved a call.

Those who worked with and for Malin Pierce frequently found it difficult to conceive of him as human. Certainly he didn't look human. The one-time Titan of the Holloway Johnson newspaper empire, founder of the greatest feature service in the lurid history of modern journalism — a feat which he was endeavoring to repeat with Phalanx for young Henry Rideout — stood about five feet ten inches tall and weighed all of three hundred and twenty-five pounds.

As he lumbered into the restaurant, his coat floated almost in opera cloak fashion about his gargantuan frame, the ends of his collar were invisible beneath the multitude of chins that supported his pear-shaped head.

"Hello, Young," he said lugubriously, his voice deep in his massive throat. That, thought Tony, was bad. When things were going to his satisfaction, the editor addressed him by his first name. Now he was showing exaggerated and ridiculous courtesy as he extended a flabby hand, added, "It was thoughtful of you to take the trouble to meet me here."

"No trouble at all, sir," said Tony, playing the game.

They moved ponderously up to the balcony. While waiting for service, the editor shook his head, making his jowls quiver madly.

"It is too bad in a way that your thoughtfulness does not extend to your work," he said, sighing deeply. "I'd come to count on you, Young." His voice grew hard. "So why did you give the story of taxi dancers clipping the soldiers to Tom Robinson over at King Features?"

"I didn't," said Tony, fighting his temper and striving to keep himself under control. "The angle was there in the original news story for anyone to see. You got it in Philadelphia almost a month ago. As a matter of fact, I was up most of the night digging out a new slant to save the yarn for you."

22

The bright little eyes twinkled alertly. Malin Pierce made puffing sounds in expression of his potential approval.

"I'm glad to hear that," he said, then sighed again. "I'm afraid our writing staff has let us down rather badly. It was in no shape to run. Why is it that men who are supposed to be good at their work — men with established reputations — seem unable to deliver for us?"

Tony wanted to reply that they might conceivably get their stories out on time if one Malin Pierce would only leave the writers alone. There was an uncomfortable silence which was saved by the arrival of the waiter with menus. Pierce, his other moods forgotten, turned his full attention on the matter of arranging to fill his paunch.

"You wait, young man," he said to Tony, "until you reach my advanced age. Dieting's no fun, let me tell you that. Waiter, listen carefully.

"First, bring me a salad — just one head of iceberg lettuce with four tomatoes, quartered, and a lemon. Then bring me three of the English mutton chops — real Southdown cuts, mind you, two pounds apiece. I'll take a double order of string beans with them and — let's see, a double order of spinach, and a bowl of dried raisins. Well, Tony, what's yours?"

Tony, who, after many meals with his editor, was still unable to believe that any man could actually stow away so much food, gulped and got in his order.

"I'll have the deviled beef bones," he said, "and a tall glass of ale."

"Where do you see deviled bones?" Malin Pierce asked abruptly, leaning across the table and twisting his fat neck to peer at his employee's menu.

"Right here," said Tony.

His employer cleared his throat thoughtfully.

"That's a fine dish, Tony. Surprised to find you appreciate deviled bones," he said. "Waiter" — in the manner of Adolf Hitler stabbing the map with his finger and impaling his next national victim — "I'll have an order of them in place of one of the mutton chops."

"The chops will take twenty minutes," said the waiter, troubled.

"That's quite all right." Pierce dismissed him with a gesture. "We're in no hurry."

"Bring my ale now," said Tony.

"Leisurely eating," began Malin Pierce eloquently, "is fast becoming a lost art. Now when I was a young man, life was better geared to enjoyment of the pleasures of the table. I remember once, when I was in Vienna with Holloway Johnson, the Archduke Franz Friederich gave us a repast that took five hours to finish. It began with the most gigantic Beluga caviar. . . ."

He continued his sermon on the benefits of not wolfing one's food until the meal arrived, when he devoured it in intense silence and with amazing speed. Over the coffee, after putting away a quadruple order of ice cream, he found his voice again. He was in far better humor, much to Tony's relief.

"I'm sorry to say," he began, "that I've just suffered a disastrous loss. My wallet, which, as you know, contains my most secret and confidential plans — "

"Is this it?" said Tony quietly, pulling it from his pocket and tossing it across the tablecloth.

Pierce stopped abruptly, stared at it in unfeigned surprise.

"Where'd *you* ever find it, Young?" he asked, his little eyes popping as his fingers went through it quickly. "Why, it's all here — money, everything!"

"I just happened to run across it," said Tony, swallowing the insult. "By the way, where'd you lose it?"

"I thought I lost it in Philadelphia last night," said Pierce.

"Are you sure you weren't in New York before the one o'clock train got in?" Tony shot at him.

Pierce turned gray.

"I don't understand," he sputtered. "Why are you

24

questioning me like this, Young?"

"Never mind now," said Tony, smiling without mirth. "I'll tell you how I found it. I went over to see an agoraphobia victim this morning in the hope of getting a story for you. Well, I found your wallet on the floor of his room in the Hotel Van Dyke. The agoraphobe's name was — "

He paused to light a cigarette. Malin Pierce, who was leaning forward impatiently, flexed his thick fingers on the tablecloth, spoke sharply.

"Come on, come on. What was it?"

"I'm not certain," said Tony. "I won't be until later. It might have been Regis Saunders. Or it might have been Curtis Lamar. You see, his face had been shot away, and I couldn't be sure."

The legs of the chair splintered and crashed as Malin Pierce's vast bulk wadded its way to the floor in a dead faint.

THE GREAT MOUND OF FLESH lay on the carpet, motionless save for a faint lifting of breast and stomach, as a hastily summoned young doctor made rapid examination. The physician, a thin, soft-spoken man, stood up at last and put his instruments away in their little brown bag.

"Dilitation," he said quietly. "He's got to be taken to a hospital at once for observation and treatment."

"How bad is it?" Tony asked.

The attack had come so suddenly on top of everything else that he was doing mental pinwheels. The doctor shrugged his shoulders.

"It's hard to say," he replied. "In itself, it doesn't seem serious — you or I would walk away and never know we'd had it. But with a man of his age and great weight — " He shrugged again, shook his head. "I'll send him up to the Lenox Hill Hospital."

Tony called Pierce's New York home — he had a place on the Drive, lived in a hotel in Philadelphia —

and gave a maid news of the attack. Then he waited around and accompanied his employer to the Lenox Hill, saw that he was settled.

It was close to four o'clock before Tony set foot again in the office. He came in half expecting Lee to tear his head right off his shoulders for being late. But Lee, it seemed, had not bothered to wait for him. He felt a moment of worried disappointment. All he needed now was to have Lee get really mad at him.

The inner office, however, was not empty. Standing in the middle of the carpet, his hands in his trouser pockets, hat back and overcoat slung open, was a thick-set, dark little man. He regarded Tony somberly as he came in.

"How're you, Young?" he said, knocking ashes from his cigarette into the tray on the desk. "Seen any dead bodies lately?"

Tony gulped, managed a miserable grin, though he felt anything but at ease. The caller was Lieutenant Phil Condon of the New York Police Department, Homicide Bureau.

"Nice to see you, Condon," he said, thereby making a thorough liar out of himself.

He turned to hang up his coat, saw the other visitor then, sitting in the straight chair back by the door. He was an enormously lanky individual with iron gray hair and a serenely wise and hard-boiled cast of countenance.

"Just a minute, Condon," said Tony, walking over to the stranger. "Who are you?"

"Are you Tony Young?" the lanky one asked. He stirred in the chair, revealing unexpectedly broad shoulders. When Tony nodded, he stood up, unraveling to a slouching six feet three.

"Malin Pierce said you needed a man," he explained. "My name is Hy Maxim. I've had plenty of experience — done my licks on the *Times*, the old *Graphic*, most of the others at one time or another. Here's a note from M. P."

26

The message, which simply stated that Tony was to put Maxim to work upon its presentation, was in Pierce's handwriting beyond question. Tony was in something of a quandary. In view of the sudden termination of his luncheon with M. P., he had, perforce, to take the truth of the note for granted.

"Come back Monday, Maxim," he said. "We need another man around here all right. I'll see what I can do."

Hy Maxim scuffed in front of him uneasily, so Tony gave him five dollars, resolving to get it back from M. P. at the first visible opportunity.

"Thanks a lot," Maxim said humbly. But there was an almost insolent lack of meekness in his eyes and manner as he shuffled from the room.

Tony turned back to Lieutenant Condon, saw the detective staring curiously after the tall reporter.

"Now what would *he* be doing up here?" Condon said idly.

Tony yawned and patted his mouth, lit a cigarette.

"One of my bosses gave him a note telling me to put him to work," he said. "Why? Do you know the long drink?"

"I used to," said Condon. He sat down in Tony's chair and put his feet on the desk blotter. "He was washed up in this town ten years ago. Faked a story and walked right into a six-figure mess of libel suits."

"Then he ought to be just dandy for this phony business," said Tony. "All Phalanx needs is a nice fat libel suit. To hell with it — what's on your mind, Phil?"

"Not much," said the detective, flicking his cigarette butt out the window with unerring aim and potential damage to any passer by on whom it happened to land below. "Guy knocked himself off in the Van Dyke this morning. Name of Regis Saunders. His daughter and Connie Talbot said a guy named Tony Young had a date for an interview with him."

"You mean that alleged agoraphobe?" Tony asked.

He hoped he sounded innocent, but had his doubts.

Condon nodded.

"He was some kind of screwball," he said disinterestedly.

"Well," said Tony, picking his words as if it were hard for him to remember. "I went over there with Carl Martin. He's my cameraman here. He's gone home for the week-end, but he'll bear me out. I was pretty leery about the yarn when Connie told me the nut had a daughter who wanted a break on the stage — the whole thing reeked of publicity.

"But we went over there. Nobody answered the door, so I said, 'To hell with it!' and Carl seconded the motion. He came back here, and I went down to the fourth floor and saw Leon Satterlee. I saw the boys were gathering in the lobby as I left, but I didn't ask them what for. I had a luncheon date coming up with the boss and didn't want to get tangled up in anything."

Condon lit another cigarette.

"Queer business," he said. "The daughter was a four-alarm pip. And the old duck was due to get cured any day now according to Doc Remsen. Still, I guess he was a psycho case, all right. Well, thanks anyway, Young. If it turns out to be anything, give me a line in the story."

The telephone rang. It was Lee.

"So you finally got back!" she said. "I found a detective and a broken-down newshound there, so I beat it with the stuff. See here, Tony. What in hell have you gotten yourself into?"

"Where are you, honey?" Tony asked.

"I'm over at Gusher's, pondering deeply on the general subject of male asininity. And I'm scared. There are a couple of men at the bar. They're watching me."

"I don't blame them," said Tony. "I'd do the same thing myself."

"Stop it, you goose, and get over here. I think they followed me from the office. Why weren't you on

28

time?"

"I'll be right over," said Tony, realizing that the girl was really scared and feeling a tremor in his own stomach. "I'm sorry to be late, but Pierce pulled a heart attack on me at lunch, and I had to get him settled in a hospital. It took time."

"Well, make it snappy," said the girl. "I've got your pay check here in my pocketbook too. They finally got in from Philly."

"Hold onto it!" moaned Tony. "I'm coming." He hung up, reached for his hat and coat.

Condon, still hanging around, looked at him curiously.

"Who was that — your girl?" he asked.

Tony shook his head.

"My secretary," he said. "She was here a little while ago."

"Yeah?" The detective blew smoke through his nose. "You didn't talk as if she were your secretary. If she's the baby that was here when I came in, I'll be back for the next show."

"Come on, Phil. Get moving," said Tony. "She's sitting on my pay check, and she's a fast gal with a buck."

He led the way from the office, slamming the door shut behind him. They parted on the sidewalk, and Tony took a taxicab east to Gusher's.

It was a small restaurant between Third and Second Avenues, unpretentious, but justly famed for its steaks, its four-ounce drinks, and for the newspaper folk who liked to cluster around its bar. Lee was sitting alone at a rear table.

"Did you find out anything?" Tony asked her.

"Shut up," she said, "and take a look at those two men at the far end of the bar. They're the ones."

Tony got a good look at their reflection in the back bar mirror, and his mouth tightened. By the way they stared studiously at their beers, he knew they'd been watching him. One was built like a barrel, and his

29

broken nose attested to violent service. The other, smaller, looked exactly as tough.

"There's a back way out of here," he said quietly. "Slip out as if you were going to the ladies' room and duck into the kitchen. I'll pick you up there."

Her lower lip trembled briefly and he saw that she was scared. An independent youngster with plenty of money in her own right, she'd attached herself to Tony a few months before, and, not being a fool, he hadn't objected. Furthermore, she'd turned out to be an amazingly able secretary — competent, cool and assured. He'd have married her in a second if it hadn't been for the fact that he already had a wife.

This was his main cross at the moment. Maebelle, the wife, had been the result of too many drinks at a press ball four years before. She'd posed as an actress — in his cups, Tony hadn't thought that strip teasing might not come under the head of the drama — and they'd galloped off to Elkton.

A commercial little tart, though unable to stick to any one man for long, she had her grappling hooks out for Tony, ready to clamp down hard on his salary whenever he gave her grounds, which put him and Lee in a wretched position.

Lee got up, once again in control of herself, moved gracefully toward the ladies' room. Tony managed to upset his chair, thus making himself the focus of all eyes in the room and giving the girl a chance to slip into the kitchen. Then, acting embarrassed, he followed her.

They raced past an open-mouthed chef, through a back door, and along an alley through the block. There Tony bundled Lee into a cab and gave the address of another small restaurant on Fifty-sixth Street just west of Fifth.

"Now," he said when they were again seated, "what is it?"

"I don't know exactly," she replied. "I can't tell you until you tell me what in hell's been happening around here. There was plenty of stuff on Curtis Lamar, but he died in nineteen-eighteen."

"I'm not so sure of that," said Tony.

He leaned across the table. Lee looked wonderful, flushed and alive with excitement in her silver foxes and the silly little hat. He kissed her.

Across a pair of whiskey and sodas, they went over the papers. Those Tony had stolen from the Van Dyke that morning consisted of a will, made out by Curtis Lamar in favor of his adopted daughter and true niece, Janet Saunders. It listed properties whose value, on paper at any rate, came to well over a hundred thousand dollars. There was also a statement of identification, into which was folded a birth certificate made out in the name of Curtis Lamar.

Lee's information, gathered from the aging news files in the library, was lengthy, running to a half dozen typed pages in single spacing. Curtis Lamar, it seemed, was or had been quite a fellow. Born with money, he'd been sent to expensive preparatory schools, finishing at Harvard and taking post graduate courses at Trinity College, Cambridge.

In London, upon his graduation, he'd attached himself to the Holloway Johnson European staff, at that time competing on even terms with the organizations of Hearst and Pulitzer for the king-pin spot in American journalism. He'd risen to the high post of executive boss of the foreign bureau, where his work, it seemed, had brought him into close contact with Malin Pierce. In fact, it had been while inspecting French forces with Pierce during World War One on the Western Front that he'd been tragically slain by a chance German bullet. The obituaries were lengthy and impressive.

"It's screwy," remarked Lee when Tony had finished reading through this mass of facts.

"It's even screwier than that, honey," he told her quietly. "This man Lamar was the man who was murdered this morning at the Van Dyke."

THREE

TONY TOLD HER THEN, in full detail, the entire story of what had happened that morning, how he'd framed the suicide, looted the apartment, been at least partly instrumental in causing Malin Pierce's heart attack.

"What," he said, "do you think I should do? The Saunders girl should know about the money. But if that Condon is onto me — and he acted just a little too smug — I'm in trouble and no fooling."

"How do my two pigeons — including the one with the broken nose — fit into the picture?" she asked abruptly, putting her empty glass down on the table with a bang.

"I don't know," he said truthfully. "In fact, what I don't know about this mess would fill a telephone book."

"I don't know why I stand for you," she said slowly. Then, her brow wrinkled with worry: "Much less why I work for you — to say nothing of getting involved in murders!"

"That's easy," he told her, managing a smile without too much difficulty. "You're mad about me. And,

strange as it seems, I'm a little that way myself —
about you." He leaned toward her, dropped his voice,
his lips less than a foot from hers. "Let's do something about it."

"Oh, Tony!" she sighed. "I'm no softy, and I do
love you — and I'm just feminine enough to get the
screaming meemies at the thought of that tramp you
married gouging both our eye-teeth out through her
shyster attorneys. I'm plenty human, but the answer
is no until we're rid of Maebelle. I wouldn't dare give
her an inch. And I'm right."

He made a helpless gesture, smiled wanly.

"Sorry, honey," he said. "I guess it's just the old
sap in my veins. Glad to know it's still there. You're
right — Maebelle's a bitch and she's out for blood and
she's smart enough to get it — but I wish to hell you
weren't and she weren't."

"Meanwhile," she said cooly, as if the interlude had
never occurred, "you've gotten yourself neatly messed
up. Condon didn't look like any fool to me. You have
no right to Regis Saunders' will, and if Condon
catches you, he'll have you dancing on a nice warm
bed of live coals. You'd better let me have it."

"Okay," he said reluctantly. "But for Pete's sake
be careful. I don't like gray suits with arrows in them
— and you wouldn't look so hot in a prison dress
either."

He handed over the loot, and she stuffed it away in
her purse. In return, she gave him his pay check.

"Take care of the drinks," she said, standing up.
"And if you still want to take me out to dinner, I'll be
home."

Tony looked after her until she'd vanished outside,
then finished his drink, got his check cashed to pay the
bill, and left. He looked at his watch, saw that it was
almost six o'clock. If he and Lee were going out
together, it was time he got home to dress.

As Tony hurried into the entrance of his apartment
house, a girl rose from one of the foyer benches and

punched a fist into his nearest bicep.

"Whoa, Napoleon," she said. "I want to talk to you."

It was Connie Talbot. Tony blinked, shrugged his wide-set shoulders.

"Come on up," he said quietly, "but don't plan to stay the night there. I'm going out to dinner." He stood aside to let her enter the elevator.

His apartment, on the eleventh floor, was large — consisting of four rooms, two baths and a kitchen. It was a rent-eating hangover from his unhappy days of married life, a living reminder of his wife's total lack of anything resembling good taste. He wished he could get rid of the white elephant, but the lease had another six months to run.

Connie Talbot flung herself down on a hideous armless sofa in a *decor moderne* of murky green fabric. She seemed entirely unaware of the fact that her skirts hiked up over her knees.

In an almost stately brunette way, Connie was a beautiful girl. Everything about her was large, but in perfect proportion. At the moment, she was wearing a passable imitation mink coat atop a black silk dress which accentuated the notably good points of her figure.

She groaned in an ecstasy of relaxation, lit a cigarette, waited in silence as Tony set about pouring the drinks.

"Make it double," she said without looking as he lifted the bottle, measuring a sizable slug of Scotch.

Tony glanced at her quickly, lifted an eyebrow, shrugged, and poured some more. She was frowning slightly, apparently lost in thought a thousand miles away.

"All right," he said, offering her the glass. "What's on your mind these days?"

She hesitated, sat up, holding the glass carefully not to spill. The scowl was still on her face as she half emptied it at one gulp.

"See here, Tony," she said finally. "I'm in a quan-

34

dary. In the first place, why in hell did you and Carl take a powder from six-o-eight in the Van Dyke this morning without taking the trouble to report Regis Saunders' death?"

Tony opened his mouth to say that they hadn't been able to get in the suite, closed it again as he saw that Connie had pulled from her pocketbook a torn piece of one of Carl's film wrappers and was dangling it in front of him.

"Seemed like too good a story to mess up with the police until we'd nailed it," he said, fumbling. "It's not often we get a chance to scoop the dailies with a Sunday supplement." He paused, conscious that he wasn't doing so well. "Look here, Connie," he blurted. "You didn't let Condon get a load of it, did you?"

"Do you think I'd still be hanging onto it if I had?" she countered. "No, Tony. Little Connie covered for her pal Tony and his pal Carl. She's just curious, that's all."

She paused, finished her drink, crossed her legs, revealing more thigh. Then she went on with her harangue.

"Little Connie wants to know why a picture of Janet Saunders was swiped from her father's bedroom, frame and all. And, most important, she wants to know why the suicide of an unknown victim of a nervous ailment should be important enough for you boys to stick your fat fannies out making a play like that. And why Regis Saunders, with life just reopening for him after twenty years of self-made jail, should commit suicide at all!"

"For Pete's sake, why ask me?" he said desperately. "I'll admit that maybe I stuck my neck out. And taking the picture was probably a mistake."

Connie Talbot inhaled deeply, blew out the smoke in a series of puffs, fiddled with her empty glass.

"Tony," she said finally, "I've known you — let's see now — for over seven years off and on. In all that time, I never saw you go off the deep end about anything except a news story — with the rank exception of the fair Maebelle, of course." She paused once more to watch Tony wince.

"But this Saunders suicide, on the face of it," she went on, "isn't much of a news story, on the face of it. I want to know what you did in that room."

The girl was breezing merrily along the highway of her deductions, hitting on all sixteen cylinders. She was literally making him sweat and enjoying it to the hilt.

"Thanks for covering me, Connie," he said, hoping against his intelligence to get her on a detour. "I don't really know what got into me up there. The old picture snatcher cropped up in me, I guess."   ·

She picked a piece of cigarette paper from her full lower lip, made a face at him.

"It's not good enough," she said. "I'm the gal who used to be a newspaperman myself — remember? And I've got a very healthy hunch that *you're* the one who's doing the covering now.

"I happen to know that your glamour-boy boss, Malin Pierce, spent last night in the Van Dyke and paid a visit to Regis Saunders. I work for the place, you know, and I can find out just about anything that happens there."

Connie turned her glass on its side and rolled it along the table cover with fingers tipped in dark red. Tony sat there and suffered.

"Old Malin tried to keep it secret — he used the too, too clever pseudonym of Marvin Poole. Subtle, wasn't he? But there's no doubt about it being him. He ate a supper in the grill that has the chef and waiters still gasping for air."

"So what?" said Tony miserably.

"So this," said Connie inexorably. "I don't think Regis Saunders did the Dutch. I think he was murdered, and you framed it to look like a suicide. You wouldn't be clamming up so tight if something like that hadn't happened. And I think you're clamming up because Malin Pierce did it and you want to save your job."

"Connie the girl detective!" said Tony. "Here, that was quite a pitch. Have another mickey."

She held out her glass without speaking, and he filled it half full of Scotch, topped it with a drop of soda. Refilling his own glass, he sat down and pondered this unexpected quirk in an already dangerously complex situation.

"There's just one thing the matter with this nice pat theory of yours," he said. For no reason he could fathom, his brain had begun to work again. "If I," he went on, "by any chance covered up a murder old M. P. committed, it would seem like a put-up job, wouldn't it?"

"I hear you talking, bub," said Connie, her eyes narrowing. "Go on."

"Well," he said, taking a sip of his drink to keep her hanging, "if it *was* a put-up job, which it must have been if your theory is right, then you were in on it in a big way. Unless memory fails me, Connie, you called me with the original tip on the story at just about exactly the time Regis Saunders is supposed to have died by his own hand. And that, my fine friend, is stretching coincidence a long, long way."

Connie set her glass, which was again empty, down on the table with a crash.

"Damn your analytical soul, Tony!" she cried explosively. "Now talk, will you? I'm not going to turn you in. Saunders *was* murdered, wasn't he?"

"Wait a minute, darling," said Tony. "Now take it easy and figure it out for yourself. *If* — and this is strictly *your* if — I found a murder in that room and framed it to look like a suicide, I'd be seventeen kinds of a demi-cretin to admit it to anyone."

Connie grinned, then came over to him and stuck out her hand. She seemed to feel that she'd won a victory of some kind.

"Thanks, Tony," she said. "You're a good guy.

You've told me all I wanted to know. And don't worry, I won't let it reach ears that will do you any harm." Then, as suddenly as it had appeared, her grin faded, and she looked worried once more.

"Maybe," she said, and Tony could read something strangely like fear in her eyes, "you told me too much." She forced back the grin, but it didn't look right. "Well, so long, Butch. It won't go any further."

"That's a relief," said Tony. "Strictly between the two of us, I'm in a worse muddle than you are. And since I've opened up for you, how about giving me a crack at the Saunders girl alone some time?"

"Alone," said Connie sweetly, "with me. She's really a swell kid, and she's all broken up about it, and I'm not leaving her unprotected to your tender mercies. She's staying with me overnight."

"I may be up to see you then later," said Tony, "if I can get away."

"That's right," said the girl, moving toward the entry. "I've heard that you're getting re-enmeshed in a female. You ought to stick with the good-time Charlottes like me. Well, I'll see you later on."

"Maybe," said Tony equivocally. He shook his head and expelled his breath in a whoosh as the door clicked shut behind her.

HE SHOWERED AND CLIMBED into his dinner jacket in a hurry — dressing for an evening out was a comparatively new phase. It had come along with Lee, who liked to wear evening gowns for the very good reason that she looked blindingly beautiful in them. When he went to the elevator, he was whistling softly to himself.

"Zoot suit?" said the liftman, a dark young Irishman named Joe.

Tony gave him a wink.

"Reet pleat, Joe," he said, grinning.

But grin and whistle faded as Tony reached the

front door. Two figures were standing against the war-darkened lamp post directly across the street. One of them, in the headlights of a passing cab, was big and bulky and had a broken nose. The other, while smaller, looked equally tough. They were the two who had tailed Lee earlier.

"What's the matter, Mr. Young?" asked Joe from the elevator door.

Tony told him with concise profanity.

"And you don't know who they are?" Joe asked.

"No. All I know is I don't want any part of them. How about letting me out the back way? I'm late as it is."

"We could try taking care of them," said Joe, disappointment in his voice. He was put together with steel cables, had the Irishman's innate love of a fight.

Tony shook his head.

"Not in these clothes," he said.

Joe rode him down to the basement, and he slipped out. Around the corner he caught a cab, went directly to Lee's.

When he entered her two-room-and-kitchenette apartment, he had to hold his breath as he looked at her. She had on a strapless white crepe evening gown he'd never seen before. Her only ornament was a gardenia in her hair, which was now upswept. He appraised her critically, shook his head in wonder.

She led him into the living room where a bottle of Fullstrength, ice, soda and glasses reposed on a tray.

"Connie Talbot just paid me a visit," Tony said.

She wrinkled her forehead at him.

"And what did the glamorous Connie want?"

"Plenty," he said, compressing his lips. "And she has plenty more doped out. I know you never liked her, but she's no dope."

"It's not that I don't like her," said Lee. "It's just that she's a woman — and at the moment, I don't crave other women around you. As a matter of fact, for my money, she's a repressed nymphomaniac, and

39

not especially repressed at that."

"You're a repressed nymphomaniac yourself," said Tony, grasping her arm and holding it tightly. "In fact, unless you've been holding out on me, you're a lot more repressed than she is, honey. And right now you're lovely enough to make me want to do something about it."

"Have another drink, darling," the girl said soothingly. Tony sighed, released her arm, let her pour the powerful Scotch for him. "You look done in, Tony," she said as she handed him his glass. "Here. Swallow this. Doctor's orders."

"We might as well get cockeyed," he said with more than a trace of bitterness. "That's about all there is for us to do the way things are."

"Damn it, darling," she said, looking at him gravely. "You know we'd be fools to start anything. We're both honestly in love, and we'd never be able to hide the fact if we — well, if we let go. And then Maebelle would move in and have grounds for collecting a fat alimony check from you and an alienation settlement from me. And just because my daddy worked hard to leave me well fixed is no reason for giving any to a bitch like her. And I'm still scared about those two heavyweights who followed me from the office this afternoon."

"You needn't be," he told her. "They've switched their attentions to me." He went on to tell her what had happened as he started over to see her.

She gripped his hand tightly.

"Tony, Tony," she said. "Damn it, *why* did you have to get all tangled up in a thing like this? It's — it's frightening."

"I didn't do it on purpose," he said, considering the amber fluid in the tumbler before him. "But somebody tried very hard to make a murderer out of old Malin Pierce. And while I don't like the old blunderbuss, I'm not going to sit idly by and let anyone get away with a thing like that."

40

"Who stood to gain anything from killing him outside of you?" she asked him. "Or haven't you thought of that? Paul Stanton and this young Rideout would have you running the whole outfit if Malin Pierce were out of the way."

"No, I hadn't thought of that," he said slowly. "But hell, anybody in the oufit might get mad enough to kill M. P. Still," he reasoned further, thinking of his colleagues, "to kill somebody else in cold blood for the lone reason of putting M. P. on the spot for murder — I dunno. There's Leon Satterlee, of course — but what he stood to gain is beyond me.

"Then there's this Curtis Lamar angle," he went on. "We've got to clear that one up before we start doping out motives. And there's Connie. She's hard-boiled enough. Not to mention the mysterious step-daughter and true niece herself. We haven't even seen her yet. Anybody else in this big city might have simply walked in there and knocked him off for reasons we know nothing of.

"Incidentally, Connie did spill one thing. M. P. spent the night in the Van Dyke and visited Saunders or Lamar or whoever he was last evening. Come to think of it, I suspect Condon's already wise to that from the way he looked when I told him the old buzzard had had a heart attack. And there you have it."

"Exactly," said Lee. "And it all adds up to exactly nothing. Come on, Sherlock, let's call crime off for the night. You have a fat roll of bills in your pocket, and I feel like shaking care."

"I'll try," he said, "but give me a quick one first. I need plenty of mechanical aid if I'm to make my mind a blank after what happened today."

He helped her into her ermine wrap, and she deliberately leaned against him while he folded it around her, then laughed at the expression on his face as she whirled away.

They did the town that night. They dined slowly, expensively, and perfectly at La Chaumiere on Fifty-sixth Street, had brandy at Twenty-one, then, in leisurely succession, visited the Savoy Plaza for a load of Hildegarde, the Persian Room, the Rainbow Room, and the Stork. Both were aware of an inner restlessness that drove them from place to place.

At three-thirty, exhausted but still unready for bed, they entered a small and excellent French restaurant in the East Fifties for supper and a nightcap. It was a quiet spot of booths and alcoves. Lee promptly slipped out of her shoes with a sigh of relief and curled her feet up under her.

"This is a swell place," she said, relaxing in the booth. "How'd you ever find it?"

"Paul Stanton introduced me to it," he told her. "It's one of his hideouts."

"That's odd," said Lee.

Something in her tone drew his attention, and he saw that she was sitting upright, her relaxation ended as she peered over his shoulder to get a better look into an alcove diagonally across the room.

"What's odd?" he asked her.

"Unless I'm out of my mind, your friend Paul is sitting across the room right now."

"No kidding!" said Tony. "He must have come back to town for the week-end." He stood up. "Hold everything. I'm going over."

He moved to the middle of the narrow floor toward the alcove Lee was watching, then stopped short and retraced his steps.

"Was I wrong or something?" she asked him.

"You weren't wrong," he said. "It's Paul, all right. And unless the camera lies, he's with the little Saunders gal."

"Damn!" said Lee vehemently. "Are we following this incredible business around or is it following us?"

"You got me there, pal," he said, sighing. "What shall we do about it?"

"We're going right over there and horn in," said Lee, fumbling for her slippers.

42

Tony blinked at her.

"Curious?" he asked.

"Of course I'm curious," she said sharply. "I'm dying to see if tragedy's daughter looks as good as her picture — not to mention what she's doing here with Paul the night after her beloved step-pappy got bumped."

He shrugged, smiled faintly, got up again and crossed the room. Lee came just above his shoulder, high heels and all. Paul looked up at him with annoyance which turned to smiling good manners as he saw the girl beside him.

"So," he said, rising, giving Tony a wink. "Miss Rankin. No wonder you told me to lay off, Tony. May I present Miss Cochrane — Miss Janet Cochrane. This is Tony Young and Lee Rankin. They claim they work in the New York office."

"Hello," said the girl pleasantly.

Tony and Lee exchanged a quick significant glance as they sat down. Janet was the Saunders girl's first name. What, they both wandered, was this Cochrane business?

The girl was an out-and-out beauty, Tony decided, of the striking, unpretty, dashingly big-featured sort who would register like money in the bank across footlights or on a movie screen.

"I know I should have kept this place a secret," said Paul, smiling. "Now I'll have to find a new hideout in order to keep the wolves away from my sheep."

"Sheep, Paul?" the Saunders-Cochrane girl asked, and all of them laughed.

"Don't worry," said Tony to Paul's girl. "I'm the one to worry, bringing Lee here in the face of Paul's artillery."

Lee ignored the talk. Her eyes were fixed speculatively on a black satin evening bag whose clasp was a rhinestone monogram forming the letters J. S. The girl noticed her gaze and smiled.

"Cochrane is my professional name," she said

quietly. "It was my mother's."

She offered no further explanation, leaned comfortably against Tony, who was sitting beside her.

"I should think something like Vere de Vere would be a better stage name," said Lee with unexpected malice. She gave Tony one of those looks though her lips were curved in the sweetest of smiles. "Or maybe Fairweather. I knew a chorus girl named Fairweather, once. She was so successful she was able to retire and live on a fat annuity in eighteen months."

"Come on, Lee," said Tony quickly, gulping down his drink.

She followed him outside, meek as a lamb.

"I'm sorry, darling," she said, hugging close to his arm. "I can't stand seeing any other woman like you."

"You'd better be sorry," he told her sternly. "The whole business of her being there with Paul was cockeyed. I only wanted to find out what made her tick."

"Don't tell me," said Lee. "I can guess from the way she acted just now."

"Shut up!" said Tony savagely, hustling her into a cab. "Around the block," he told the driver. "Pull up at the corner."

"What are you going to do now?" Lee asked curiously.

"I'm not sure, but it's just about closing time," he told her. "Have a cigarette and shut up."

They didn't have long to wait. Paul and the Saunders girl emerged in a few moments, and Tony was surprised to notice definite unsteadiness in Stanton's gait. He hadn't appeared intoxicated in the cafe. But something had evidently hit him, for the Saunders girl took him home first. She certainly didn't seem especially cut up over her adopted father's sudden demise.

However, the blonde did not go directly back to the Van Dyke, where Connie Talbot was supposed to be putting her up. Instead, she was driven east on Forty-

second Street, past Pershing Square to a rough looking bar between Second and Third Avenue. Her
driver waited for her there with motor running. Tony
had their cab pull in just beyond the Third Avenue
intersection.

"Stay here," he told Lee. "I'm going to reconnoiter."

"Be careful," she told him. "I'm really scared."

He left his opera hat in the car and turned up his
coat collar so his white muffler wouldn't show. Then,
carefully, he looked in the barroom window.

He could see the girl's back, her blonde hair agleam
above the white fur that topped her black evening
wrap. He had to wait for a minute or so before he
could get a look at her companion. She dropped her
bag, leaned over to pick it up, and he found himself
looking directly at Leon Satterlee.

"What the hell!" he muttered as he walked back to
the cab.

Then and there he made up his mind to pay Connie
Talbot a visit despite the lateness of the hour. He
told Lee what he had seen on the ride back to her
apartment, omitting, however, all mention of his
immediate intentions.

"I'll be up for breakfast tomorrow afternoon — this
afternoon, rather," he said in the foyer of her apartment house.

"Come up for a moment, won't you?" she pleaded.
"I'm sorry I was bitchy."

"My nerves couldn't stand it," he told her. "To say
nothing of my self-control. Honey, if you don't break
down soon, I'll be in a loony-bin." He kissed her
quickly, roughly, and was gone.

TONY LOOKED AT HIS WATCH and shook his
head. It was getting uncomfortably close to five
o'clock — a hell of an hour to go calling. But there
were still things to be done, and it was already Sunday, when the subject of his visitation could sleep it

off. He taxied to the Van Dyke, picked up a house telephone in the vacant lobby, and succeeded in rousing a sleepy night operator sufficiently to put a call through to Connie Talbot's room. Rather to his surprise, she answered promptly.

"Sure, it's all right," she told him. "Come on up, Tony. I've got to talk to you."

When he arrived a moment later, she was wearing a semi-transparent light blue negligee. It seemed to him that she came unnecessarily close to him and held his hand a lot longer than she needed to for a mere hello.

He wondered what the hell. For the pure animal attraction of the white flesh that revealed itself all too clearly through her robe was extremely potent.

In trying to figure out the setup, Tony couldn't help wondering if she hadn't set the stage for him. He debated the point as she moved across the room to a tabouret on which were a half empty cut-class decanter of whiskey, a fizz bottle, and several glasses.

"Here, Tony," she said, holding out a filled glass whose color was suspiciously dark. "Have a little drink."

He accepted it, eyed its deep amber hue dubiously. It certainly didn't look little.

"Haven't got any ice," she said with a flipper-like gesture of one soft arm. "Sorry, but the more I drink, the more British I get."

"Where's the Saunders girl?" he inquired, sitting down on the sofa. "I thought you told me that she was spending the night with you here."

"I thought so too," she said. She shrugged twice, lifted her glass and drained it. "How should I know?" she went on. "When I got back from your place this evening, she was gone. And little Connie's been sitting here all night — all by herself.

"All by herself, Tony — and that ain't right. 'Snot good for little girls to drink all by themselves."

He tasted his highball and nearly did a back somer-

46

sault. It was virtually straight whiskey. He choked back the retch that shook him to his heels, tried to figure this out. But the answer eluded him. Connie, while a two-fisted, hard-drinking girl, was notorious for her ability to stay sober or at least upright after absorbing vast amounts of alcohol.

But she was certainly plastered now. At the moment she was sprawled in an armchair, revealing the inevitable length of thigh, her head nodding, her eyes almost shut. For a horrible moment, he feared she was going to pass out on him before they could talk. But no. With sudden, swift determination, she sat upright, took a deep breath and literally shook herself sober.

"Tony," she said crisply, "I've been bilked, swindled, left on the road — little Connie, who's supposed to know her way around in this man's town." She paused, beat the arm of her chair with an angry fist.

"No fooling, Tony, I've been pushed around like a Daisy Mae from the hill country. And little Connie's going to get even. She doesn't like it. And somebody else is going to like it a whole lot less. Tony — and get this now — I know who killed that poor Saunders man. I know all about it!"

Tony sat up and took notice. He couldn't quite decide whether she was telling the truth or suffering from delusions of an alcohol-fogged brain.

"Who was it?" he asked in a mixture of patience and eagerness.

She shook her head and wagged a playful finger at him.

"Connie's going to tell you," she declared, "but first she's going to tell you *why* she's going to tell you."

He stifled a groan,. began to figure on a quick getaway. But more out of politeness than any belief in her deductive capacity or information, he asked her why.

"It's like this," said the girl, and her head wagged unsteadily. "Little Connie's going to tell you because you've got a right to know. You're the person who put her finger onto it in the first place."

"*What!*" he snapped, startled.

This was totally unexpected. His mind raced back over their conversation, and he tried to dope out what in heaven's name he could have revealed.

"Remember," she said thickly, "when you told me that if this murder was a put-up job this morning, I had to be in on it?"

He nodded, and she pulled herself upright and swayed to the tabouret. There she poured herself another knockout potion, almost drained it at a gulp.

"Well," she said, running her tongue over her lips as if to be sure that no drop escaped her, "that broke it. I came back here and thought it over for a while. And then I needed a drink. Little Connie needed a drink the worst way. Because Little Connie knew what had happened once she put her mind to it. Little Connie had been played for a solid sucker!"

This was becoming unbearable. Tony took a false pull at his impossible highball. If she didn't get to the point soon, he'd go crazy.

"Okay, Connie," he said with a smile he hoped looked real. "You're a swell tomato to tell me all this. Who in hell did murder the poor old man?"

She held up one finger, wagged it sagely, a cross between a jitterbug and a marionette. She nearly fell, regained her balance by a quick grab at the back of a chair.

"You take it easy, Tony," she said. "Wait right here. Little Connie has something to show you, and it will tell you everything she knows."

She stumbled through the bedroom door, slammed it loudly shut behind her, nearly catching the train of her negligee in it. Tony rose and stamped up and down the living room, puffing furiously at a cigarette.

For a while in the next room, he could hear Connie slamming things around. She seemed to be having trouble with a bureau drawer, evidently pulled on it too hard, for it came out all the way with a crash after a series of rasping pulls. Then, as the seconds ticked away, no noise at all came through the solid old hotel wall.

Tony grew more and more restless. He wanted to get home to bed — Lord knew it was time — but he didn't dare. Connie might well have some information, might not feel like giving it to him once she's sobered up.

It was all too evident that she was in some sort of an emotional state. If that dizzy dame had passed out — and she was obviously on the rim of a collapse, had been when he came in — well, he'd have wasted his time. He toyed with the thought of going in after her, finally made up his mind to do it, took a pair of determined steps toward the door.

Then, from the bedroom, came the most appalling scream he had ever heard. He stopped short, frozen. But finally, forcing himself to action, he tore the door open, stepped inside. A door into the other corridor at the far end of the bedroom was also open, and in it stood Leon Satterlee. His eyes bulged, his head was thrown back, and his mouth was wide.

From it came horrible animal shrieks. They began with a gurgle, rose like a siren, faded to a rasping half cough. A pink bubbly froth appeared on his lips and Satterlee fell forward on his face, lay there writhing and kicking and twitching.

It was then that Tony saw the cause of his seizure. Connie Talbot lay on the bed. Her eyes were staring right at him, but they weren't seeing him or anything else. The little trickle of crimson that ran slowly from the inner side of her left breast made that all too evident.

Connie Talbot was dead, shot, murdered. Tony had a vivid recollection of the sound he'd believed to be the crash of a bureau drawer on the floor.

Sounds of protest and general coming-to-life were audible in the corridor, so Tony pulled Leon Satterlee all the way into the room, shut the door and left him there. He loped back to the living room of the suite to telephone.

"Get me Lieutenant Condon — Homicide," he snapped.

"What's going on up there?" an indignant operator inquired. "I've had thirteen calls — "

"Murder!" said Tony brutally. "Get Condon."

He managed to prevail upon the headquarters switchboard operator to put the call straight through to the detective, who was home in bed.

"This is Tony Young," he said.

"Listen, you drunken bum — " began the sleepy officer.

Tony cut him off. Someone was pounding at the door now, and he had to make it brief.

"Now *you* listen," he said. "I got a call from Connie Talbot to see her about that Saunders suicide. So I came up to her room to talk. She told me it wasn't a suicide, said she knew who did it, went into the bedroom to get proof. She was cockeyed, but making sense in a way. I heard someone scream, broke in and found her shot dead and Leon Satterlee standing in the other door having himself a first-class fit and yelling his head off about it. Get over here, will you?"

"Coming," said Condon, hanging up.

Tony put the telephone back on its cradle, looked up to see a frightened Negro elevator operator in the doorway with a small cluster of white faces and curl papers gathered behind him.

"Tell those people to get back in bed," he snapped at the liftman. "Unless they've seen something."

Condon made amazingly good time. From his appearance, Tony judged he'd put on most of his clothes in a taxicab. His vest was buttoned unevenly, and he was minus a tie. He came in quickly, paused to look inquiringly at Tony, who nodded toward the bedroom.

"I've let Satterlee stay put," said the latter. "I figured you'd want to look around alone before any doctors or harness cops began hashing clues."

50

Condon grunted, took a look in the other room. Then he stepped inside, closing the door behind him. He was back within five minutes.

"Call the house doctor," he said. "Tell him to come to the bedroom door and drag Satterlee out by the heels and find out what's biting him. Stay where you are, Tony."

Tony picked up the phone. From the use of his first name, he gathered Condon was grateful to him for contacting him direct instead of reporting the murder through usual channels.

"One thing, you," said Condon to the elevator man, who was still hanging around. "What's that elevator across the hall from the bedroom door?"

"Lemme see," said the colored man. "That *used* to be the freight elevator, but it's too old. Nobody uses it now. It's locked."

"That," snapped the lieutenant, "is what you think. Wait outside to help the doctor if he needs you."

As the liftman left, Tony put down the phone, retrieved his half empty highball glass from the floor beside the sofa. He didn't mind the strength of the drink any more.

Condon returned to the bedroom, again shutting the door. He was gone perhaps ten minutes this time. When he returned, he picked up the decanter and poured a stiff jolt into an obviously unused glass.

"Now," he said to Tony, "the boys will be here in a moment. You and I have got to have a talk alone. So far, I can't see you as a killer, but you're in it to your ears."

"Thanks," said Tony quietly. "I'll tell you what I can. I'm beginning to think my being in it can't be entirely coincidence. But I can't dope it out any other way yet."

"Where do you think we ought to talk?" asked the detective.

Tony looked thoughtful.

"It might not be a bad idea to have a conference in

Leon Satterlee's room," he suggested with a faint smile.

Condon looked surprised, then grinned one-sidedly.

"It's a thought," he said. "We might even — oh, here are the boys now."

He opened the door, and half a dozen policemen walked in, accompanied by headquarters technicians and a doctor from the medical examiner's staff.

"Go over the joint," Condon told them. "I'm stepping out for a bite. Come along, Tony."

Walking down to Room 428, Tony could hear the detective humming cheerfully over his shoulder. He wondered why Condon should be feeling happy with a double killing on his hands, then remembered that murders were the detective's life work.

He stood aside at the door, and the lieutenant put his hand on the knob. It refused to turn. He yanked at it, then pushed. The door opened so easily that he stumbled in off balance.

"Busted!" he said laconically. "Now what in hell could that mean?"

Tony found the light switch and turned it on.

"I'll be damned!" said the lieutenant.

The apartment looked like shredded wheat. The floor was knee deep in papers, index cards, photographs. The cardboard files had been ripped open ruthlessly or overturned, the steel ones jimmied out of shape.

FOUR

TONY PUSHED BACK his hat and surveyed the wreckage. "What in hell did this — mice? No wonder Satterlee threw a fit. These things were his life."

"Yeah, I know," said Condon. "What a sweet job of sorting out this is going to be! See here, Tony, I'm going to have to stick around here and do some spade work — at least get a decent search organized. Why don't you scram along home and cut yourself some sleep? Wait there for me tomorrow. I'll get over late in the morning."

"I'll be there until noon," said Tony. "After that I'm going over to Lee's for breakfast. Good hunting, Phil."

He was so tired as he staggered out and reeled into a taxicab that the end of each of his millions of nerves seemed to cry out on its own complaining pitch. He sank back against the leather cushions and closed his eyes. When at last the vehicle pulled to a stop in front of his apartment house marquee, the driver had to lean through the partition and shake him back to consciousness.

Tony paid him off, stood rather stupidly on the curb,

stretching and yawning, when he caught sight of the two men approaching him silently.

They were the same pair who had followed Lee from the office, had later tried to trap him as he left his apartment. Damn! Why hadn't he remembered them and gone in through the back alley? As he sleepily tried to collect his thoughts, the smaller of the pair got between him and the door. The big one with the broken nose came warily up to Tony, his eyes agleam.

"Are you Mr. Young?" he asked.

Instinctively Tony nodded, and the man's hand streaked inside the lapel of his coat. With sudden complete awakening, Tony decided to his horror that they meant to gun him down right there on the sidewalk.

He lowered his head and charged. Broken nose, apparently not expecting such a move, was caught with his hand still inside his coat. Tony's head hit him squarely in the diaphragm, knocking the wind out of him and sending him staggering back into a hydrant against the wall of the building. Broken nose tripped over this, banged his head against the bricks and stumbled, moaning, to the concrete.

Tony found himself yelling at the top of his lungs as he swung to face his second opponent. But he pivoted just a trifle too late — and walked into a right hook that made his head blaze and ring like a bell. From the force of the blow, Tony could have sworn his jaw was broken, and he wondered how such a comparatively little fellow could pack such a stiff punch.

It was then that he saw the brass knuckles. With a whoop of alarm, his head still fuzzy, he began to retreat. The hoodlum, ugly and angry, moved after him, lashing out with an occasional fist.

Tony didn't like those knucks. They kept getting too close to his face for comfort. He ducked, tried to get room for a good old football charge, but the man crowded him constantly, wouldn't give him leeway. He felt the wall against his back, knew he was cornered, barely dodged a particularly vicious swipe.

He lashed out with his feet, aiming for his man's shins. It wasn't sporting, but neither were the knucks. The man cursed and sobbed as Tony drove a hard leather toe against the thin skin over his tibia. Tony jumped at him, trying to get on top of the metal-shod fist and wrap it up, got a sickening blow in the breastbone in return. He staggered back, weak as a kitten, feeling that he was going to be sick. This was it, he decided. He couldn't fight any more.

"Scram, Heinie!" shouted the big tramp, who had managed to get his feet back under him though his head was a ball of blood.

Joe, the elevator lad, appeared on the scene in his shirtsleeves, carrying a heavy monkey wrench. The toughs faded fast around the corner.

"You okay, Mr. Young?" Joe asked.

"Yeah." Tony managed to gasp as he lost a complete three-fifty dinner on the curb. "Sorry, Joe. And thanks — for getting out here. I was done. Fellow had knucks."

"The lice!" said Joe. "I wish I'd gotten here in time to take a crack at them with this" — he looked at the wrench longingly — "but I was taking a nap in the cage and didn't hear you hollering until a moment ago."

"You did all right, Joe," said Tony leaning against a lamp post. "Take me upstairs, kid. I want to get to bed."

He had just taken off his coat with fingers still weak and unsteady and was examining four neat little bruises along the line of his jaw where that first punch had landed when the telephone rang. It was Condon.

"Are you alone there?" the detective asked. "You haven't got Malin Pierce up there, have you?"

"Wait a minute," said Tony. "One of us is nuts. I told you I took him to the Lenox Hill Hospital after lunch. He had himself a heart attack. And I just got slugged up pretty by a pair of hoods."

"Cut it out!" groaned the detective. "I've got too

55

much on my hands now. Oh well — give it to us."

Tony told him all he could, which did not do much to clarify the already involved situation. Condon swore succulently.

"What is this about M. P.?" Tony asked to break it up.

"Well, heart attacks are pretty funny things sometimes," said Condon. "Take this one your boss just had for instance — he got right up after his supper and walked out of the hospital without even kissing the nurse good-bye."

"What am I supposed to know about it?" Tony asked. "I gave up trying to predict M. P.'s movements a long time back."

"Well, we're asking everybody," said the detective. "We haven't been able to locate him yet. And that human monstrosity has got to be somewhere."

"Don't worry, Phil," said Tony. "You'll dig him soon enough. And the old tub of butter's not here. So long."

He hung up slowly, passed a hand over his eyes. What with strain, fatigue, and the slugging he'd just taken, he had a headache that was a beautiful thing in itself, but not in his head. When he took his hand down and opened his eyes, he blinked in disbelief.

A squat, monstrous figure was filling the door from foyer to living room. Puffed purple lips were curled in a sardonic smile without causing the half chewed cigar in one corner of the flabby mouth to tremble. Tony put his hand back over his eyes and counted to ten.

"Maybe you'll be gone when I look again," he muttered.

"I regret," Pierce said in his most unctuous manner, "to be forced to inform you that the — old tub of butter as you so succinctly put it — has imposed himself upon you to the extent of making you a liar to the police."

Tony didn't say anything. There didn't seem to be anything to say. But as he gazed into the little clownlike eyes, he became aware of a far from subtle change in the personality of his editor.

At best — if you could call anything about this incredibly difficult and fantastic personality even good — Malin Pierce was always a creature of quick-changing moods, turning them on and off like a veteran stock company character man. But he wasn't acting now. And Tony felt a shiver ride up his spine at the open malevolence of that expression.

"What are you doing here, M. P.?" he asked, moving into the living room and watching his boss squash himself into a chair. He sat down himself, shakily.

"I merely wanted to have a short conversation with you — that's all," said Malin Pierce softly. Then he roared, "Stop this holding out act of yours, Young! If you want to keep your job with Phalanx, tell me what happened to this Saunders story."

Tony did a quick mental evaluation of the cards in his hand. Pierce, he felt, was either bluffing or was colossally ignorant. He decided to play his game slowly.

"What," he countered quietly, "were *you* doing in Saunders' room last night? What were you doing at the Van Dyke at all? What was your wallet doing in Saunders' room? And what have you been doing this evening since skipping out of the Lenox Hill?"

He was allowed to complete this series of questions only because the rage which was suffusing Malin Pierce had apparently rendered him speechless. He huffed and puffed for a full ten seconds before he was able to speak at all.

When the storm finally broke over Tony's aching head, it was almost incomprehensible — save for the redundant fact that Pierce considered him annihilated and erased as an employee of Phalanx. Tony waited, smoking a cigarette without comment, until the tornado had used up its own momentum, then shrugged weary shoulders.

"I haven't asked you anything the police won't be

asking you tomorrow," he said disinterestedly.

This statement reversed the field. Malin Pierce began to tremble, his mouth fell open, the disgustingly chewed cigar hung unlit from his pendulous lower lip.

"Just a minute, young man," said Pierce. "What have the police to do with this?"

"Am I fired?" Tony asked.

Pierce sighed, closed his eyes, opened them quickly. He made a helpless gesture with his pudgy hands open.

"No, Tony," he managed to say, and the latter could see that every word was torture to his ego-maniacal boss. "You know better than that. I couldn't replace you if I wanted to."

"Very well, M. P.," said the younger man. "When I get through with this, you may feel different again. Regis Saunders or Curtis Lamar or whoever he was was murdered. And your wallet was left on the floor by his body.

"*I* — get this — *I* framed that murder to look like a suicide to save your ungrateful hide. By the way, M. P., if you have a revolver, check on it. In view of the pocketbook being there, the gun might turn out to be yours too."

Malin Pierce passed a shaking hand over his sweating forehead.

"Go on," he said.

"In view of all that's happened since," said Tony, "I'm very much afraid that the suicide isn't going to stick. Connie Talbot, the girl who handles — handled, rather — the publicity for the Van Dyke, was aware of what I did from the first. She was murdered, almost before my eyes, a few minutes ago because she'd figured out who the killer was or thought she had. And I'm afraid you'll have to dig up some pretty solid alibis for yourself. The police are sorer than hell."

Malin Pierce closed his eyes again, and for a moment or two Tony was horrified lest the older man should have another attack here in his apartment. However, he opened them after a bit, and Tony saw that his boss

58

had merely been concentrating. He asked for brandy, and Tony went out to the kitchen and got him some, the tail end of a fine old Napoleon 77 Lee had given him on his birthday. Pierce drained a glass, set it down, smacking his lips.

"Excellent, Tony," he said, nodding toward the bottle. "I really came up here to ask you something else entirely. Where is the girl now?"

"The girl?" Tony stared at him. "Oh, you mean the Saunders kid, I take it. I don't know."

He decided to leave it at that. Telling M. P. that she had been with Paul Stanton would undoubtedly lead to further trouble. He thought of something else.

"How did you get in here?" he asked. "You're not exactly inconspicuous, M. P., and after my telling Condon you weren't here, it's going to mean woe."

For the second time, Pierce smiled — an idiotic, conceited little smirk. He waggled a fat finger at Tony.

"I don't believe you'll be troubled," he said. "I merely called up a friend of long standing in the profession of journalism and obtained a list of residents in the building from the reverse telephone directory. Then I called on a Mrs. Brown who lives two floors below, said I was expected, and walked up from there." He dangled a ring of extremely odd keys in his hand as he spoke.

Then the pleasure faded quickly from his face. He put the master keys away and stood up. Tony let him get his own coat. The young man was so angry he didn't trust himself to speak. Condon would never be fooled by such a stupid gag, and, if he reported the visit to the police, he'd be out of a job. It was the old squeeze again with himself in the middle. He grunted as Malin Pierce paused on the threshold to wave farewell.

"It was loyal and considerate of you to try to arrange things for me," said the editor pompously. "I'll give you more concrete assurance of my appreciation when I return to Philadelphia."

As soon as he'd gone, Tony, cursing to himself in a low but efficient monotone, stripped off his evening clothes, poured himself hurriedly into gray flannels, packed a few things in a bag, and went downstairs in the elevator. Thanks to Pierce, he felt certain that sleep in his own place would be sketchy at best.

"If anyone wants me," he told Joe, "I'm ferrying a bomber to Africa. See that the day men get that message too. And thanks again for saving my neck."

He slipped the youngster five dollars, hailed a cab and told the driver to take him to the Grand Savoy near the Plaza. The gray of early morning made the city look tired and ill around the cab as it moved uptown.

WHEN TONY WOKE UP, his head ached, and his eyes were stuck together, and he felt as if he had hardly been asleep at all. As soon as he was able to see, he looked out the window of his hotel room, saw to his astonishment that it was darker than when he'd gone to bed.

Had he slept through the entire day? No, not if his watch was correct. The dial read eleven-thirty, and if it were Post Meridian, the room would be darker still. Then the rapid drip of rain on the sill of his open window told the story. It was not yet noon, and he hadn't had very much sleep. He groaned with self-disgust and pity, turned over and sought more slumber. But slumber had gone out for the day, it seemed. Finally he gave it up and called Lee.

"Darling!" she cried. "I've been terrified. I couldn't get you at home. Where in hell are you?"

He told her. "Come on over," he said, "and bring all the beer in your icebox. Thanks to the Sunday laws, I won't be able to get any here until one o'clock."

He called police headquarters next and told Condon where he was, to that authority's mixed relief and disgust. With a tremendous effort, he got out of bed and staggered into the shower. He was in dressing gown and trousers when Lee arrived, lugging a heavy brown paper bag. She looked half angry at him as she put the bag down with a satisfactory plunk of glass.

"Connie Talbot was knocked off last night," he told her as he finally got the bathroom bottle opener working.

She gasped a little as he handed her a bottle.

"Tony! It wasn't in the paper!" she said.

"It broke too late," said Tony. "I went up there after I left you to try and find out the why of the Saunders gal's movements." He went on to tell her of his hectic session at the Van Dyke. "I knew you'd be worried," he concluded, "and I didn't want to spoil your sleep by scaring you any more."

"You didn't want me to worry!" she said derisively. "I've only been trying like crazy to find you since nine o'clock. Why didn't you call me before?"

"Come here," said Tony.

He pulled her down on his lap and kissed her soundly. She gave a little cry that was half sob and returned his embrace. Then she lay against him, her head on his shoulder.

"I'm going after Maebelle," he said suddenly, "and get myself out from under that female sword of Damocles. I don't know about you, but this is torture for me."

"I'm not made of granite," said the girl. "But be careful what you do with Maebelle. She'll have your hide off if you give her an opening. You'd better be plenty sure you've got something on her first."

"That isn't very chivalrous," said Tony.

"I'm not going to marry any knight in armor with an alimony rap hanging over him," said Lee. "Damn it all, darling, this whole lousy business has me scared silly."

"You're not the only one," he said, grinning and tousling her hair again. "I'm plenty scared myself. Connie's murder last night, coming right on the heels of the Saunders murder, didn't leave me feeling any too secure. And then those two guys who tried to beat me up — say, you're a pip, can't you see my wounds?"

"I thought they were lipstick and was being tactful enough not to say anything," said Lee. Then she grew serious, demanded and got an explanation. She looked tense and blue-lipped when he'd finished.

"They might have killed you!" she said. "I won't have it. I'm going to find those two and . . ."

"Okay," said Tony. "But you should see how *they* look today. By the way, what did you do with the loot I gave you?"

"I put the papers into an envelope and sent them to Miss Janet Saunders at the Van Dyke," she told him. "I printed the name and address and just dropped them in a corner mail box."

"Swell," he said. "You couldn't have done better. Now what about the watch and picture?"

"I stuffed them down a sidewalk gutter at Forty-fourth Street and Seventh Avenue," she said.

He heaved a sigh of relief and grinned.

"Listen, honey," he said abruptly, "I've got an idea."

"That has a familiar ring," she said philosophically, "and sounds like more work for Lee. Sometimes I wonder why you can't keep your mind on other women like a normal man."

"I try," he told her. "But a fugitive thought just popped up. Suppose the Saunders girl was telling the truth when she said her mother's name was Cochrane. Be an angel and see if any Cochranes turn up in the files."

"Spend Sunday in the library!" she exploded. "My answer in four words is to hell with it!"

"But Condon's due over here any second now," he informed her. "I think it would be a lot smarter for me to see him alone. I'll get up to your place just as soon as he's gone. Now be a good gal and scram."

She stuck her tongue out at him. "Okay," she said grudgingly, "but for God's sake be careful with Condon. I don't think I'd like the smell of the Tombs."

When the door had closed behind her, he went to the telephone and asked for the Sunday papers and more cigarettes. He had just finished with the comic section when Condon arrived.

The detective looked entirely fagged out. He stretched full length on the unmade bed. Tony handed him a bottle of beer, which was accepted gratefully.

"Nothing makes sense," growled the detective, shaking his head. "A nut commits suicide. A press agent thinks it's murder and promptly gets herself knocked off. Another nut has a fit. Your fat boss has a fit of his own and then vanishes. The suicide's daughter takes a powder on her own."

"Et cetera," Tony added. His forehead grew wrinkled. "Look here, I'm going to give you something. You'll want to break my neck, but try and see it from my angle. When I finished talking to you on the telephone last night, old M. P. in person walked out of my bedroom."

"I wondered how long it would take you to tell me that," said Condon, smiling faintly.

"You knew?"

"Of course I knew. A big barrel of lard like Pierce is about as inconspicuous as a bass drum. We know he was at your place, but we lost him after that. Where'd he go?"

"I can't tell you," said Tony, "because I didn't ask him. Hell, Phil, I've got a job to hang onto."

"That's what I figured," said the detective. "Now, how about giving me an idea of what you two talked about?"

Tony went over his conversation with Pierce, omitting, of course, the fact that he'd told M. P. about turning the Saunders murder into an apparent suicide to keep the fat man out of a frame-up.

"By the way," he asked Condon in conclusion, "whose gun did kill Saunders anyway?"

"Pierce's," said Condon quietly. "Ballistics and registration check. And, incidentally, it wasn't a suicide. Somebody knocked him off and stuck the gun in his hand — we gave the hand a paraffin test and learned that it hadn't fired any six-gun."

Tony felt suddenly chilly. He wondered how many fingerprints he'd left scattered around the bureau.

"There's another queer thing," the detective went blandly on. "That service elevator. It's in perfect working condition, though it hasn't been in official use for years. And the only oiled-up door is on the seventh floor. At the bottom, it gives on the service alley."

"What do you know about that!" said Tony, really surprised. "Who killed Connie?"

"I'm pretty sure you didn't," said Condon, "and that goes for your girl friend too. And I'm pretty sure Satterlee didn't, though I'd give a month's salary to be able to get him to talk sense. He's as hysterical as a woman going through the change. So far, we have no clues. But hell, anybody — even Pierce — could have come up in that elevator, done the job, and beat it."

Tony nodded. He was trying desperately not to appear over-nervous.

"What about the wreck of Satterlee's apartment?" he asked. "Did you find anything there?"

"Prints," said the detective. "Hundreds of them — all alike. A man's, and I'm not including Satterlee in *that* category. But they aren't on record."

"So what happens?" Tony asked.

"So we hold our water until something breaks," the detective stated gloomily. "Something will, all right, with Pierce and the Saunders gal still running loose. You keep plugging, Tony. And if anything happens, you know how to get in touch with me."

"Okay, Phil," said Tony as Condon got slowly off the bed and set his now empty bottle on the floor. "Since you've learned so much," he said, "I suppose you know all about the two gorillas who tried to slap me around last night — this morning rather."

"Weren't you kidding?" asked Condon, apparently honestly perplexed.

Tony showed him his bruises, gave him the story. Condon sat down again heavily, looked as if he wanted to bury his face in his hands.

"That's all I needed," he said bitterly. "A pair of apes who go around tailing people or beating them up with no explanation offered. Maybe I'd better put a man on you."

"Not me," said Tony. "I'll be careful."

"You'd better be," said the detective. "What a mess!" He lifted a hand in farewell and stalked out wearily.

The hotel room seemed to Tony to grow smaller with each tick of his watch once the detective had departed. It was only a little after noon — damn! He thought longingly of his liquor cabinet at home. But that was still out of the question. He had neither desire nor intention to be a clay pigeon for the police reporters who were undoubtedly maintaining a vigil outside his door.

Then he recalled the bottle which was nestling snugly in a drawer of his desk at the office — a bottle of good whiskey. The more he thought of it, the thirstier he became. Finally, on sudden impulse, he threw down the Sunday paper, hurried into his clothes.

A light gleamed through the ground-glass outer door window as he left the elevator and walked along the corridor. Tony paused to think this phenomenon over as he selected the key from the bunch in his pocket. Who in hell had forgotten?

Then he recalled that the lights had not been on at all yesterday. His next thought was that the police might be giving his offices a search, and he had a moment of panic as he remembered the pictures of Saunders' corpse before and after he'd moved the gun into its hand.

His lips tightened as a third possibility entered his thoughts. Suppose the mysterious killer or killers were in there, trying to learn how their plans had gone wrong. Well, to hell with it, he was going in.

He thanked the Lord for the carpet which kept his footsteps silent. Yes, the door to the inner office was open, and the light came from there. With his stomach doing nip-ups, he wished he had a gun with him, looked around a bit prayerfully for a weapon. He took a short bar of wood, used during the summer months to prop up one of the windows which had a stubborn sash. On tiptoe, he moved along the wall and peered around the edge of the partition.

A rangy, rather attractive looking young man was sitting at his desk, apparently going through all his papers. The drawers were pulled wide open, and the top of the desk was piled high with their contents. To his unspeakable rage and anguish, Tony saw his precious bottle, its contents appreciably lowered, resting beside the intruder's elbow. With a low growl, more of pain than of anger, he stepped inside, his window jack balanced to deliver a crashing blow on the vandal's skull.

"What in hell do you think you're doing here?" he barked.

The young man look up, surprised. He had black, close-cropped hair above a wide, intelligent forehead, a face both sensitive and powerful, whose single blemish was an extremely crooked nose. At Tony's approach, he leaped to his feet with a yelp and hastily thrust one of the extra chairs between them.

"Just a minute," he said deprecatingly. "Who are you?" There was something in his voice and manner, and sense of authority, that made Tony hesitate and half lower his improvised weapon.

"I happen to be in charge of this office," he said. "And furthermore, that happens to be my whiskey — and those are my papers you're reading."

"So *you're* Young," said the stranger. He grinned and extended his right hand. "Sorry about the whiskey, but I had to go to a banquet last night and can remember feeling better. I'm Hank Rideout."

TONY RAN A HAND through his hair, tossed his improvised weapon into a corner and managed a foolish grin. There was nothing else he could do. Hank Rideout, old Jeremiah Rideout's only surviving son, was the big boss, the man Paul and M. P. took orders from.

It was their first meeting, and Tony thought that for a man who had handled successfully over a period of two years great newspaper organizations in Philadelphia and Chicago, a flock of trade papers and magazines, and innumerable affiliated interests, Hank Rideout looked unexpectedly young. At the moment, the tycoon's expression was one of unadulterated curiosity.

"Am I crazy, or did you play football at Princeton some time back?" he asked abruptly.

"I held on for a couple of seasons until they got wise to me and kicked me out," said Tony. "Why?"

By way of answer, Rideout put a finger to his bent nose. Under the pressure, it squashed flat against his face, revealing the absence of cartilage beneath it.

"Remember the Cornell game in 'thirty-one?" he asked.

Tony, still puzzled, nodded slowly.

"Well," the young newspaper owner went on, "I don't — at least nothing after the opening kickoff. But they tell me you're the guy who hit me on the first play. I was out for two hours. I didn't associate you with the Young in the New York office."

"I'll be damned!" said Tony. "I guess I didn't like the Cornells that year." He reached for the bottle and took a healthy pull at it, then handed it over to his employer. "What brings you to these parts?" he asked.

They sat down, both a trifle self-conscious, and lit cigarettes. Tony found himself warming to his visitor and judged by the look Rideout shot at him that the feeling was mutual.

"Frankly," said Rideout, "I came up to New York to talk turkey with Pierce and Stanton. Stanton came back from the road with a terrific report on sales yesterday, but when I looked at the magazine Pierce got out for today, it stank. So did the magazines for the last six weeks when I looked them up. And that doesn't jibe with Stanton's report. And I hate things that don't jibe."

"See here," said Tony uncomfortably. "I'm in no spot to talk about it, even to you. Those two wolves have been squeezing me like a teddy bear between them for months."

"I can see that," said Rideout dryly. He nodded toward the papers from Tony's desk drawers which he'd been going over. "I've been combing your carbons. By the dates on those letters and the material in them, it seems to me that we should have been at least a week ahead of all the other supplements for months.

"But in spite of this material you've been sending down to them, we're running a good two weeks behind King and the rest. Yet down in Philadelphia, they've been blaming their slowness on you."

"The rats!" said Tony, though he was anything but surprised. The syndicate business was dog eat dog. Therefore, he was glad to have Hank Rideout's ear alone for a bit — especially since the big boss seemed so regular. "But them's kind words anyway. Are you seeing Pierce and Stanton in this office? I'd like to bury some of that stuff you've been looking at if you are."

"No," said Rideout, shaking his head. "I'm having a talk with Paul Stanton up at my place in the Languedoc Towers tonight. This visit was just a spur-of-the-moment idea. If I've offended by snooping, I apologize."

"You haven't," said Tony. "I'm glad you've had a

look at the real score. You're paying for it, you know."

"Yes," said Rideout, looking slightly pained, "I'm paying for it." He grinned ruefully. "By the way, I'm giving a little party up at the Towers tonight. Why don't you come up? Bring somebody with you if you have a date."

"Thanks," said Tony. Then he chuckled. "Have you gotten in touch with M. P. yet?"

"No," said Rideout. "No, I haven't yet. Why?" He looked at Tony curiously. "What's so funny about it?"

"Just this," said Tony. "If you do run across him, you might call Lieutenant Condon of the Homicide Bureau and let him know. He's looking for M. P. too."

"Good God!" said Rideout. "What is this — a joke?"

"No," said Tony, his smile fading. "It's no joke."

He went on to give Rideout a detailed account of what had happened since the morning of the day before. The young newspaper owner's brows rose several times, but he asked few questions. At the finish of the account, he shook his head slowly.

"That's not so good," he said. "No, I don't mean your part in this mess, Tony. Hell, you've only stuck your neck out a mile to keep old M. P. out of trouble. Don't let it throw you. If I do find Pierce, I'll let Condon know — that his name? — Condon?

"Okay," he went on as Tony said it was. "If the old boy's a murderer — and I don't for a moment believe it — we can do nothing to help him. And if he isn't, we can get him out of this mess. But before we go on with it, I wish you'd tell me what *you* think of Phalanx and its chances for success. I've sunk a lot of money in it already."

There was something almost wistful in the young millionaire's tone, as if he found it impossible to get the truth out of anybody. It was, thought Tony, the penalty of being born to seventy million dollars.

"Hell," Tony told himself. "He's a good guy, and the money isn't his fault, and I owe him something for busting his nose."

So he gave it to him straight.

"Phalanx as it now stands," he said quietly, "is one more in an inglorious process of attempts to found newspaper syndicates that have wound up in the boneyard. It has a life — but not under the present set-up — and I'm not counting the war as a vital factor in its potential ruin."

"What *do* you think is wrong?" asked Rideout. He was frowning as he listened, drawing little squares within squares on a piece of white copy paper.

"Malin Pierce is chiefly to blame," said Tony, keeping his fingers crossed and feeling like a prize heel for telling on his immediate chief. "He is thoroughly cracked up from his gross over-eating and can't even keep the swing of daily assignments going. In other words, he can't do his job as it should be done — and, worse, he's so afraid one of his staff will show him up that he won't let any of us do any work either. I hate to say this. It's probably just because he's old that —"

"Don't start that, Tony," said Rideout. "He's got plenty of money salted away in one form or another — even enough to carry that 'gross overeating' you just mentioned. Now keep going."

"Paul Stanton wants Phalanx to succeed," said Tony, "but he's still thinking in terms of the *American Weekly*. I've seen it happen again and again. The *American Weekly* succeeded as no other publication in history — no one has ever gotten nineteen thousand dollars for one full-page ad, and, I might add, gotten them in the number that Arthur Kobler succeeded in attracting during his heydey."

He paused, took another pull at the bottle. Rideout followed him, then both of them lit fresh cigarettes.

"The trouble is that those days — at least as the Hearst gang lived them — have gone forever. They were based on selling the public three kinds of stories — those based on religion, sex or buried treasure. They hit the fundamentals.

"But the public is getting more sophisticated. That's only natural after the load of quack mysticism, phony erotics and something for nothing they read for years. Worse, every attempt to copy the *Weekly* has been just that — a copy, therefore necessarily not as powerful or able as the original.

"Paul thinks we can do it — I haven't disagreed with him, but the poor issues we've been getting out are a perfect proof of my point. It can't be done."

"That sounds reasonable," said Hank, "if not very pleasant." They had another drink. "I suppose," he went on, "that you have a few ideas of your own about making Phalanx show a profit."

"Now," said Tony, "you're talking my meat. I'd like to get some figures ready to prove my points before I throw them at you too hard, but I can give you a general idea. As the supplement field is divided today, the top of the scale is occupied by *This Week* of the New York Herald Tribune, which puts on a pretty fair imitation of a slick weekly magazine.

"At the other end of the scale, the *American Weekly* still reigns supreme — followed by Tom Robertson's *Saturday Magazine*. For the rest, the syndicates sell individual pages to be purchased as desired by various Sunday papers. And that's about all there is.

"If you're a highbrow or a slick magazine regular, you'll do well on Sundays. And if you're a cross between a cretin and a haemosyphalic, you can turn to the cheapies. But if you're a normal middle-class American, you've got no magazine to read on Sundays. There's a gap between the top and bottom of the field you could drive an armored division through without firing a shot and —"

He broke off abruptly and cocked an ear. Someone has moved through the outer door to the elevators. He'd heard the latch snap as the door swung to.

"There's been somebody in here," he said, and moved hurriedly toward the hall.

Hank Rideout followed close on his heels, but even as they came out into the reception foyer, they heard the elevator gate close.

Tony hesitated. There was no use in trying to chase the intruder now. Only one elevator was in service on Sundays. But the building's street door opened directly beneath his window, five stories down. He raced back to the inner office and peered out. Rideout stayed at his side.

The street was virtually deserted in the pelting rain. In a few moments a tall man with an arrogant slouch swung around the corner and moved north up Fifth Avenue.

It was Hy Maxim, the strange reporter with the unpleasant record, who had arrived with a recommendation from M. P. the day before. Tony indulged in some plain and fancy swearing.

"We've been overheard, all right," he said to Hank.

Tony went on to explain the little he knew of the one-time ace reporter. Then, on sudden impulse, he went along the inner corridor to Carl Martin's darkroom. Under the blue glow, it looked as badly messed about as Leon Satterlee's apartment had appeared in the early hours of the morning. Tony's remarks were vitriolic.

"Take it easy, Tony," said Hank Rideout, putting a hand on his broad shoulder.

Tony stopped swearing.

"*I* don't care so much," he concluded. "But Martin is just as temperamental and hard to handle as any other photographer, and when he gets a load of this mess, he'll be really wild."

He swung on Rideout then, a sudden thought striking him.

"By the way, Hank," he inquired, "how did *you* get in here?"

Rideout looked puzzled.

"I meant to ask you about that, but it slipped my mind in the light of the extraordinary things you've

72

had to tell me," he said. "The door was unlocked. I didn't like it."

"The son of a gun must have left it unlatched yesterday!" exclaimed Tony. "He must have snubbed it to open when he went out. And I just slammed it shut. Damn!"

"I've got to run now," said Rideout. "I'll look forward to seeing you tonight."

"If I'm not in jail," said Tony gloomily. Then he grinned at his own despondency, and they shook hands.

"I'm glad we finally met face to face," Rideout concluded. He pressed his broken nose again and laughed. "It begins to look as if certain elements must have been doing their damnedest to keep us apart."

FIVE

TONY WENT BACK TO the telephone in his own office and tried vainly to reach Lee. He was long overdue for his date with her. But despite three dialings, her telephone refused to do more than sneer its lack of interest at him. Finally he sat down and put his feet on the desk and took a lugubrious pull on the by now almost empty bottle. It was already dark outside, and the street lamps were on, making gloomy reflections on the rain-soaked pavement.

He let his mind dwell again on the weird behavior of Hy Maxim. Here was an angle of the case he had lacked both time and opportunity to explore. What in the world could he have been trying to accomplish by messing around in Carl's developing room?

Those pictures of the corpse! The shots he'd had Carl take of the Saunders body as a murderee and then as a suicide! Thank God Carl had taken them home — or had he?

That was something else to worry about. At any rate, it went a long way toward showing that Maxim was somehow tied up in the murders.

Tony finished the bottle regretfully, tried Lee's apartment on the phone again — and again failed to get any response. All at once, he began to worry about her.

There was a murderer loose. Suppose somehow he'd gotten wind of the girl's library investigations, had grown fearful of her digging some long-buried clue out of the files — well, the thought curdled him. He shuddered, tried to pull himself together, took a vain pull at the bottle — and nearly lost a tooth by jumping six inches as the telephone shrilled unexpectedly at his elbow.

"Tony," said Lee's voice, and it was oddly flat and a bit breathless. "Get over here to my place quickly!"

"Coming," he said. "I've been burning the wires trying to reach you. Is anything wrong, honey?"

"Well," she said needlessly. "I'm home now — and nothing's wrong. Just get over here as fast as you can paddle." The receiver clicked sharply in his ear.

Thanks to the wretched weather conditions and the usual week-end snarl around the Queensborough Bridge approaches, it took his cab almost fifteen minutes to make the twenty-five odd blocks to Lee's apartment. She greeted him with subdued excitement, led him triumphantly to the center of the living room carpet.

There her gaze directed his vision to a weeping, crimson-eyed Hy Maxim who, trussed by a clothesline, lay writhing on the sofa. A large bump, purple and ugly, showed through the disheveled hair on top of his head.

"My God!" breathed Tony. "I thought you said there was nothing wrong up here. What in hell goes on?"

She gave him a bright smile, pirouetted across the room to stare insultingly at her human prize.

"Does it look as if anything were wrong?" she said proudly. "I did it with my little slipper."

"Let me just get this pepper out of my eyes,"

groaned the ex-reporter savagely, "and I'll give you both something to remember me by. *Ooooow!* It's murder!"

"It's not pepper," said Lee, evidently entirely pleased with herself. "It's a very expensive shade of Chanel face powder. I'd hate to taste it in a Welsh rarebit.

"Tony," she went on, "I was forever at the library. When I finally got back here, somebody — you can guess who — called me on the telephone and told me that you wanted me to come over to the office right away.

"That didn't make sense, so I marched out and marched right back again. I found *him* here just sneaking into my bedroom — imagine? — so I did a little sneaking on my own and came up in back of him and took off my shoe and let him have it. I didn't like him anyway — from the time he came into the office yesterday."

"What about his eyes?" Tony asked. "You didn't put powder in them with a slipper."

"Give me time," said Lee, taking a cigarette from the box on one of the end tables and lighting it unhurriedly.

Maxim groaned again, and she prodded him with a sharp toe where it would do the most good.

"I tried to drag him over to the sofa, but I guess I didn't hit him hard enough — anyway, he came to and tried to wrestle. I had to do something, so I got my compact out and blew the powder into his eyes. Then all I had to do was lead him over here and push him down and tie him up. He was like a lamb."

"Some lamb!" said Tony. In spite of the danger of the situation, he failed to restrain a grin. Lee looked so entirely feminine and helpless beside the lank masculinity of the ex-reporter. "Never mind, honey," he consoled. "I'll buy you a new compact. You're terrific!" His smile faded as he turned to the ex-reporter.

"Okay, Maxim," he snapped. "Now tell us what in

hell you thought you were doing in Miss Rankin's bedroom."

"Ask her," said Maxim, speaking through clenched teeth.

Lee shook her head.

"I don't get it," she said. "I found the files, but there were too many of them to finish today, so I persuaded the librarian to let me bring them home. Though how this triple-barreled rat found out about my being there today is more than I can figure out."

"I can," said Tony quietly. "He was listening in while I gave Hank Rideout the whole story at the office just now. He must have legged it right over here. We saw him go, but couldn't stop him."

"Try and prove that!" shouted Maxim.

"I think we can safely let Lieutenant Condon take care of that little item," said Tony.

With an unfriendly look at the bound Maxim, he went over to the telephone, dialed police headquarters.

Maxim took that moment to make a sudden convulsive movement. Leaping like a landed carp, he sprang from the sofa to the carpet, the clothesline unraveling about him as he struggled out of its toils.

"Dames make bum sailors!" he said, ramming a hard, bony shoulder into Tony's diaphragm.

Tony tried to swing the telephone down on his head, but he'd been caught off balance, his wind knocked out, and he went down in a tangle with the phone wire and the small table.

"They can't tie knots!" yelled Maxim.

He gave Lee a shove that sent her spinning into the wall. One long leap took him along the foyer to the hall door.

By the time Tony had untangled himself from the telephone wire and table legs and discarded clothesline and recovered something of his wind, pursuit was out of the question.

"You look sick, darling," cried Lee, coming over to him.

He waved her away, clutching at his diaphragm.

"Just my wind," he said, and did some fancy swearing. "I'm all right. Call Condon."

Lee got the lieutenant on the wire and gave him a report on what had happened.

"He says he'd like to have talked with friend Maxim," she said to Tony. "He'll be over soon."

"Okay," said Tony, beginning to feel better — good enough to waive the drink which Lee offered him by way of a restorative. "Now, honey," he continued, "what did you dig up on the Cochrane dame that drew that long cockroach over here in such a hurry?"

"It's in here," she said, moving to her bedroom.

She came back bearing a block of folded sheets of paper, half a dozen magazines and a couple of books. Tony relieved her of it, dug into it, and emitted a whistle of surprise.

Janet Cochrane — the original Janet Cochrane — had been, it seemed, a spectacular, in fact, almost a notorious figure in the theater of thirty years ago. She had been one of the first girls of any social standing whatever to risk the public damnation that went side by side with a stage career in those days.

"Look at this," said Lee, covering the page he was studying with the yellowed double spread of a primitive Sunday supplement of long ago.

BEAUTY AND BRAINS UNITE!

Beneath this cryptic headline, well larded with lithographic art in faded but still raw colors, was a lengthy account of the wedding of Janet Cochrane — at the conclusion of a spectacular two-season run in a Broadway musical show — to Malin Pierce, brilliant young executive editor of all the vast Holloway Johnson journalistic empire. The date was November 17, 1916.

Reading further, Tony's interest now fully awakened, he was informed that Miss Cochrane, with her marriage, was retiring from the theater forever. Also revealed for the first time, the paper said, was Miss Cochrane's true identity, which had been religiously concealed because of her family's eminent position in society. Miss Cochrane was, in truth, or had been before her marriage, Janet Lamar, whose brother, Curtis, had also shocked society by turning down Newport and Wall Street for the thrills of journalism, becoming associated, as was the groom, with the multifarious Holloway Johnson interests.

There was more — later stuff. The birth of the baby, Janet, in 1917, was next. This received quite a play from the press, which took the opportunity to rehash the earlier stories of the courtship and marriage.

From that point on, however, the notices were few and brief. Early in 1918, Mrs. Malin Pierce had once more pioneered for her sex by being among the first women to use Reno for the purpose of divorce. Except that her charges included extreme cruelty, little detail was given.

"Has it occurred to you, darling," Lee said, after waiting gravely until Tony had finished reading the clippings, "that the next lap in the story, save for Janet Cochrane's suicide in 1919, is the death of Curtis Lamar in France?"

"It seems odd that of all people, M. P. should have traveled abroad with Lamar just then," said Tony. "I'll grant you that. Evidently his cruelty was more than just his wife's imagination — but hold on!"

"I thought you'd get it sooner or later," said Lee. "Really, darling, you're so terribly clever that sometimes I wonder — "

"Stow that," said Tony. "How can we prove anything? All this does — if Saunders was Lamar — is make poor old M. P. out to be the killer even more than before."

The doorbell rang and Lee hurried to answer it. Condon came in. Tony thought for a moment of trying to conceal the Cochrane story, but Condon was already on the edge of the carpet, eyeing the library loot with a half smile on his tired face.

"Now tell us about Maxim," he said.

Tony gave him all the gory details, and when he'd finished, the lieutenant scowled and shook his head. He didn't look happy.

"Outside of his effort to break in here," he stated, "we haven't a thing to hold him on. You'll have a hell of a time proving he was snooping around your office, Tony, if he has any kind of an alibi."

Tony nodded, then showed the detective the material Lee had dug up in the library files. Condon accepted a drink gratefully, sipped it while scanning the copy.

"Who would the Pierce girl be now?" he inquired.

The gleam in his eye hinted that he already knew the answer. Tony told him of meeting Janet Saunders the night before and the JC monogram on her handbag. Again Condon shook his head.

"For Pete's sake, Phil," said Tony, "we give you all this hot stuff we dig up on our own and you shake your head!"

"Pipe down," said the detective. "I've got so many suspects now that I can't pin this thing on anybody. And every bit of new stuff that's turned up has just made it that much tougher. By the way, Tony, you don't know anything about Connie Talbot's love life, do you?"

"Sorry," said Tony. "She kept her own affairs pretty quiet."

"Well, that elevator boy at the Van Dyke says he used to take time off his job around midnight and smoke a cigarette in the back alley. About half a dozen times he saw a man walk into the hotel and disappear. Remembering that trick elevator, I think he may have been little Connie's boy friend."

"How much of a description did they give you?" Tony asked.

"What's the matter, Tony?" Condon asked, smiling. "Got a bum conscience?"

Lee hissed the detective, and both men smiled.

"They didn't give me much," the lieutenant went on. "Just that he was of middle height and always wore his overcoat collar up and hat brim down. They couldn't tell whether he was fat or thin except that he wasn't terribly fat. He kept to the shadows and never spoke to them. And that was that."

"It sounds like half of New York," said Tony. "Well, Lee, we're going to a party tonight."

HANK RIDOUT'S NEW YORK RESIDENCE atop the Languedoc Towers was a physical and esthetic hangover from the days when there were still untaxed Titans in America's moneyed circles. Built by his father, the fabulous Jeremiah Rideout, the place spread over the three top floors of the huge apartment hotel, complete with terraces, ballroom, a banquet hall, a music salon and a conservatory.

To Hank, it was a tax-eating white elephant of the worst sort. Not naturally inclined to live on the pompous and lavish scale its use implied, he kept but one floor open, employed that only when he had to entertain in New York on a large scale. However, one floor was more than enough.

There were people there that Sunday night — all sorts of people. Tony recognized more or less notable characters from the ranks of the newspaper world, from upper-case race-track circles, from the canyons of finance, radio folks, advertising writers, sporting celebrities, and a liberal larding of Broadway. This last was especially noticeable among the girls, most of whom were pretty, a few beautiful, and only a sparse handful obviously wives.

Tony and Lee walked in shortly before midnight, just as the party was getting into full cry. After a couple of happy encounters with champagne-bearing flunkies, they turned simultaneously to look into their host's smiling face. He was wearing a dark lounge suit, though some of his guests were in white ties, and there were uniforms everywhere.

"This is Hank Rideout, honey," said Tony. "Hank — my fiancee, Miss Rankin — otherwise Lee."

"I'm sorry it's just this kind of a jam," Rideout said pleasantly. "But I wanted to see Tony, and I couldn't very well put it off. Most of the boys and girls here like this sort of thing, and I have to toss one every so often or have them calling me a stuffed shirt."

He waved at some new arrivals, blew a kiss to a rouged and over-jeweled elderly lady. Then he slipped an arm through each of theirs and spoke in low tones.

"There'll be another little party in a few minutes," he said. "Just a few people will be there. I want you both to come. I'll need you both." His smile widened again, and he passed along after beckoning to a waiter.

"How do you like him?" Tony asked as she sipped her drink.

Lee grabbed his arm, nearly spilling both their glasses, held onto it tightly.

"Golly!" she said. "He seems swell. That was pretty grand — what he said about wanting to see you. I'm excited — *Tony!*"

But he was gazing across the room, his eyes wide, his lips parted, a slight frown on his brow. Lee followed his gaze, saw a plump girl who, in the almost but not quite vain belief that she had a Petty girl figure, was poured into a gown of scarlet satin that brought every curve of her opulent figure into high relief.

The dress clashed violently with the bright henna of her hair, which floated loosely around her shoulders. She was talking loudly and with gestures to a circle of males, hanging on the arm of an over-handsome youth with a thatch of waved yellow hair that looked like a toupee.

"My God!" muttered Tony. "It *is!*"

"*It* is what?" asked Lee.

Tony came out of it, flashed her a wry grimace.

"*It*," said Tony, "is Maebelle, my spouse, believe it or not."

"*Tony!*" cried Lee. "It isn't! How *could* you?"

"It's neither long nor complex," he replied. "You see that *corpus non delicti* of hers — well, even you'll admit it has a certain elemental appeal. And she wasn't wearing clothes like that. She's the kind who looks a lot better without any."

"She's probably more at home that way," said Lee sweetly.

Tony gave her a look, then shook his head.

"Have your fun," he said dismally.

"You've had yours, I take it," said Lee.

Somehow, her heel came down sharply on his instep. He winced.

"Cut it out," he whispered. "She sees us. She's coming over. Smile, pussy, smile."

"Tony, *dear!*" said Maebelle, calling from halfway across the room and drawing everyone's attention. She still had the blond youth in tow.

"Tony, I've been trying to find you everywhere," she said, her voice still loud. "Where have you been anyway?" She cast a meaningful look at Lee, who stood her ground womanfully.

"You can't have looked very hard," said Tony. "I'm still hanging out in the same places."

"But I *have* been looking," said Maebelle. "You see, I want a divorce. I want to become Mrs. Lavery — this is Lavery. Smile, Pat." She pushed blond-thatch forward, where he mumbled something about being charmed.

"And this," she went on, beaming at Lee, "must be the little girl I've been hearing *so* much about. Tony, you always were a naughty boy. I really don't blame you this time — she's *sweet!*"

Lee began muttering viciously to herself, and Tony stepped on her foot for a change.

"Miss Rankin — Mrs. Young and Mr. Lavery," said Tony. "So you really want a divorce, Maebelle?"

"I've already started proceedings, darling," said Maebelle. "That's why I've been trying to find you. In view of the things I've been hearing, dear, I'm sure we won't have any trouble being civilized about agreeing to disagree?"

"Don't be too sure, Maebelle," said Tony. "I still have a fancy for my eyeteeth."

"Dear Tony!" cried Maebelle with a silvery laugh. But her eyes were venomous.

Lee yanked Tony away. "Of all the lousy, dirty, oversexed, gold-digging little tramps!" she murmured in his ear. "Why in hell did you ever do it, Tony?"

"For Pete's sake!" said Tony. "Take another good look at her. She was made to do it *with*."

"I couldn't hold my cookies if I took another look at that would-be Theda Bara," snapped the girl, "and I'm not talking about your sex life. I want to know why you married her."

"So do I," said Tony. "Honestly, Lee, it was one of those things."

"Anything wrong?" Hank Rideout's voice asked.

Lee promptly looked sweet again, and Tony shook his head.

"Everything's fine," he said. "Couldn't be better."

"The private party's started," said Rideout. He led them along a hall lined with Venetian mirrors framed in gold. "By the way, Tony," the young millionaire said over his shoulder, "you spoke of certain figures you offered to get up for me this afternoon. How soon can I have them?"

"Tomorrow," said Tony quietly, his personal troubles forgotten. "If this rash of murder doesn't claim me as its number three victim, I can get the whole works up in rough fashion in two undisturbed hours."

"Swell," said Rideout. "I'll be ready for them as soon as you can give them to me."

They paused outside an elaborate carved oak door,

which the publisher opened for them. A comfortable lounge with open fire burning and wide French windows looking out onto a colonnaded balcony and overlooking Central Park lay before them.

Phil Condon, glass in one fist and cigarette in another, got slowly to his feet and smiled a greeting as they entered.

"Don't be surprised, Tony," said Rideout quietly. "Thanks to our little talk this afternoon, I realized that, apart from the victims themselves in this one-man crime wave, I'm likely to suffer most. Close to a million dollars has been sunk in Phalanx already, and it's got to come back. So I thought we'd better go over things."

"Mr. Rideout says he has a couple of angles," said Condon.

The others sat down and Rideout cleared his throat.

"My father, as you may or may not know, was circulation manager for all of the Holloway Johnson enterprises until nineteen-twenty. He left the organization in that year to take over his own newspapers.

"At any rate, for years he was very friendly with both Malin Pierce and Curtis Lamar. Naturally, I only knew in the vaguest way of the trouble that developed between those two over Lamar's sister and her unfortunate marriage to Pierce.

"But — after her death, Dad took the little girl in. Pierce, at the time, was abroad, and the Lamars wanted no part of the child. So there was no one else to take care of her. Unofficially, she took our name, and I took her for granted as one of the family.

"Her relatives made no especial effort to take her away. She became a sort of kid sister to me. Then, while I was away at school, my father died. I came home for the funeral and found Janet had vanished. Once again, no one told me anything about her. After a while, it slipped into the back of my head, though I didn't forget her."

He paused, saw that everyone was supplied with

drinks and cigarettes before going on with his story.

"Last year," he resumed, "Pierce came to me with his scheme for Phalanx. Things were going well generally, and I was about ready to branch out, so I listened. My memory was clouded with his greatness in years gone by, and he can still bend anybody's ear.

"So Malin Pierce came back into my life. And, just two weeks ago, I received a curious letter. It's in my vault in a Philadelphia bank, but I believe I can give you an accurate resume of its contents." He lit another cigarette.

"It stated that the writer knew the whereabouts of Janet," Rideout went on, "and that she was not too well off, and that if I'd meet him in a certain place, he'd like to make a deal for the information. It was unsigned. I may have been a damned fool, but it stirred up a lot of old memories, and I kept the date. I met the writer in a second-rate hotel in a Philadelphia side street." He turned to Tony. "The man who met me was the man who ran out of your offices this afternoon."

"Maxim!" said Tony.

Rideout nodded, and Condon quietly got up and crossed the room to refill his glass.

"He informed me that Janet was Malin Pierce's daughter, but that her uncle had adopted her and was living with her here in the Van Dyke in New York. He said they weren't too well off, that she wanted to go on the stage but could not because of her adopted father's strange affliction — gave me the whole story, in short.

"Naturally, I went directly to Malin Pierce. After all, the girl was his daughter. It was his right to do whatever had to be done for her comfort. I thought the old devil would collapse—oddly enough, or at least it seemed odd to me then, he look terrified. However, he agreed readily enough to make the negotiations.

"But he didn't do anything about it — in other words, he began to stall. And I wanted to see Janet again and help her if I could. So I put Paul Stanton on it — and Paul got results. Just a moment, please."

Rising, Rideout picked up a telephone in the corner of the room and spoke into it softly. Returning, he spread his hands, palms outward.

"Because of a friendly, if possibly egotistical desire to help someone I hadn't seen in years, I seem to have started a crime wave single-handed."

Condon shook his head.

"It wasn't your fault," he said. "A case like this that runs way back into the past is hell to figure. Confidentially, we've got Pierce spotted. We should have a call on that any minute now."

Tony was puzzled. He still found himself unable to make a murderer out of Malin Pierce. With his own child involved, however, it might well have happened. Men have done strange things where the welfare of their offspring was concerned.

His train of thought was broken by the opening of the oak door. Janet Pierce-Cochrane-Lamar-Saunders stood there, with Paul Stanton at her shoulder.

She was no longer the gayly theatrical person of the night before. Her face was pale, her eyes circled, her manner tautly nervous. But she was still a beauty, clad in black, her hair a stylized reminder of her mother's Gibson Girl coiffure. Smiling faintly at Lee and Tony, she moved gracefully to Rideout, who took her by the hand and introduced her to Condon.

"I remember you," she said, "the other morning." She spoke gravely and steadily. "I'm sorry if I've caused you any worry, but the chance to slip away was too much for me."

Tony ached to ask her what she'd been doing with Leon Satterlee in the Forty-second Street bar, but a look at Rideout's expression of pride in her restrained him.

"Lieutenant," she said unexpectedly, "you're holding a man who's been helping me to find my father's murderer."

SIX

"ARE YOU SPEAKING of Satterlee, by any chance?" inquired the detective.

Tony rather envied the lieutenant his smiling poise, knowing that he must be thoroughly angry with at least two persons in the room — for keeping the girl's whereabouts under cover for twenty-four hours.

"How did you know?" Janet Pierce-Cochrane-Lamar-Saunders asked, evidently startled.

Condon raised his eyebrows, then, much to Tony's relief, shook his head. He didn't want the detective telling the story of the night before. It would make for unpleasantness if Paul Stanton learned that he'd been followed the night before.

"As a matter of fact," said Condon, "Satterlee is locked up in a private hospital. When his files were torn apart, he broke down completely. I'd be greatly in the debt of anyone who could get him talking coherently."

Tony marveled at the courtly way in which Condon used the ten-dollar words for the occasion.

"I'll give you the address if you want it, miss," the detective went on. "I was afraid that if I turned him over to the regular city psychopathic ward, they'd have him hanging from palm trees and tossing coconuts in a week."

"Thank you for your consideration," Janet Pierce said simply. "I've been half frantic myself for fear something more serious had happened to him. I believe he was really about to discover who killed my stepfather — the fact his files were raided is pretty good proof of that." She nodded further thanks as she took from the detective the card on which he'd inscribed Satterlee's address.

"We may be able to save you a visit to him," said Condon, grinning one-sidedly. "You see, we already know that —"

The telephone rang then, setting up answering clamor in more than one set of overtired nerves. Rideout took the call, held the instrument to his ear, listened silently for a moment, then handed it to the detective.

"For you," he said.

Condon took it with a slight nod, listened for a full half minute after making himself known to the person on the other end of the wire.

"Okay! Swell!" he said then. "Bring him up here right now," he remarked with enthusiasm into the mouthpiece. And, turning to the others, "They've just picked up Malin Pierce. Since almost everyone concerned in the case is present — if Mr. Rideout doesn't mind — we'll hold our hearing right up here."

"It's all right with me," said Rideout. "There's a special elevator in the side entrance that comes directly to the hall here."

"We know about that too," said Condon.

Tony, who had been paying close attention to the interplay, was diverted by a whisper in his ear.

"Tony," said Paul Stanton, putting a hand on his shoulder, "it's beginning to look as if you're about to be the new white-haired lad in Phalanx. You made a big hit with Hank Rideout, you dog."

It made Tony feel a little sick. Not that it wasn't entirely true, especially since his talk with the young millionaire that afternoon. But he was climbing into his first really big-league job because old Malin Pierce was going to be charged with murder.

"How'd you manage to find Mr. Pierce?" asked Lee suddenly to the room at large.

Condon smiled again, this time almost sincerely. But his manner was self-deprecating.

"It's not a thing to be especially proud of — not in the way of police work," he said. "We simply looked him up and found he has a place up on Riverside Drive — he has a ninety-nine-year lease or something. We put a watch on the place. When we checked the maid's marketing orders and found that she was buying enough food for ten people instead of the three that make up the staff, we figured we didn't have to look much further. So we got a warrant and went into the house tonight. Pierce was hiding in the cellar."

No one said anything for a full minute. Tony accepted the champagne a butler came around with. Hank Rideout and Janet of the many names made places for themselves on the sofa. Lee and Condon remained in their places, while Tony and Paul stood near a portable bar at the far end of the room.

Two detectives broke the spell then when they came in with Malin Pierce bulking immensely between them. Condon dismissed the plainclothesmen with a curt nod of his head, examined the monstrous human hogshead cooly. Pierce was apparently in a terrible state of sheer blue funk.

"Well, Mr. Pierce," said the lieutenant quietly, "don't you think it's about time you offered us an explanation of your conduct the last few days?"

The fat man nodded dumbly, his frightened eyes darting around the room. They finally came to rest on Paul and Tony.

"So you sold me out!" he barked, fear vanishing before the onset of one of his professional rages.

"Never mind that!" snapped Condon. "You're talking to me."

Pierce subsided like a pricked balloon, and his gaze rested on Janet. "You too?" he said tragically. "My own flesh?"

The girl said nothing, turned her golden head away.

"Mr. Rideout," Condon cut in, this time with finality. "You may stay or not as you wish. But I think the ladies had better go outside. You too, Mr. Stanton. Tony, I want you here."

"I'll wait outside," said Hank Rideout gratefully. "Come on, Janet."

Paul and Lee and the butler followed them to the door, where their progress was interrupted by an inrushing detective.

"Listen, Lieutenant," he said, his voice low but excited. "This Satterlee is here. Says he's got to see you."

Condon swore lustily. "Here I've been waiting all day for the dope to open his mouth," he complained, "and the screwball comes busting in at the one time I *don't* want to see him. Who let him out of the booby-hatch anyway?"

"There's an attendant with him," said the plain-clothesman.

Condon shrugged wearily.

"Okay," he said. "He may have to wait a while. But don't let him in here or out of this place until I give you the word."

The three of them were finally alone in the room with the doors and windows closed. Condon lit a cigarette, and Tony finished his wine. Pierce remained standing in the middle of the carpet.

"Sit down, Pierce," said Condon, his voice gentle. "You must be tired."

He had turned his back on the editor, putting his match in a tray, but wheeled suddenly as the creaking mass of blubber was in the act of lowering himself into a chair.

"*Yeah!* Tired from running away!" he barked.

"I had to run!" Pierce croaked, panic returning to bulge his eyes. "Somebody's after me — wants to kill me. They've killed two people already, and I'll be the third."

"Get wise to yourself," Condon sneered. "You've been working this game yourself — with one accomplice. And I know who he is."

"You're lying!" cried Pierce. "All I wanted to do was get my daughter back!"

Condon let his manner grow patient, turned his back once more, walked to the other end of the room.

"Come on, Pierce," he said when he returned. "Let's quit stalling. You can't get out of this. You're done — finished!"

"You're mad," said the editor.

Condon stopped looking patient.

"Listen, Pierce," he began, his voice iron. "You thought you killed Curtis Lamar in France during the last war. He lay in a shell hole for three days and was out of his mind when a French ambulance unit brought him in. When he did come to, he couldn't bear exposed places — the shell hole had meant safety.

"Meanwhile, you'd announced his death. You believed he *was* dead — until a few weeks ago you heard he was alive. For twenty years, you'd forgotten you had a daughter — and then all you wanted to do was get the man who'd taken care of her out of your way.

"You went to see him in his rooms — rooms he couldn't leave because of you. You fought again, put your alleged brain to work. You called Connie Talbot, told her there was a story in the hotel she could use — and you used it too as cover for murder.

"You knew Satterlee alone outside of yourself had the whole story. You got Satterlee up there right after you'd killed your one-time brother-in-law and made it look like suicide. And then you let your own daughter and Connie Talbot discover the crime."

"That's not true," said M. P. He no longer sounded desperate, merely tired.

"Oh, no?" Condon poured it on. "At that, if you hadn't made a couple of mistakes, you'd have been okay. First you swiped some documents in case they incriminated you, then had the nerve to send them back. You also forgot that Miss Talbot was bound to add it up — so you had to kill her.

"And then you remembered Satterlee's gossip files and the possibility that Young, here, and Martin might have gotten wise and gotten some pictures. So you gave your accomplice the job of cleaning out the files and the laboratory of your own New York office."

The detective paused, came to where Tony was standing by the portable bar, poured a hooker. Tony kept his eyes on the editor. Pierce's expression had become bland. His eyes were back to their normal slits, and from a pocket he fished up a cigar on which he chewed like a happy cow.

"Just a moment," he said, chuckling. "If I killed Lamar — which I didn't — why in hell would I have involved Connie Talbot?"

"You tell me," said Condon.

"I have never," said Pierce, "to my knowledge, met Miss Talbot, much less murdered the unfortunate young woman."

"*She* knew *you*," said the lieutenant.

Pierce glanced down at his incredible stomach with a faint smirk. "Who doesn't?" he asked.

Condon swore.

"That was a nice point you made about Satterlee," Pierce resumed. "If, as you say, I killed Lamar, if I'd even known Satterlee, I might have done it. Or, as you also suggest, delegated that task to an unfortunately non-existent accomplice."

He paused to twist his cigar to the other corner of his mouth.

"Who, by the way," he asked, "is this mysterious

co-worker?"

"You tell him, Tony," said the weary lieutenant.

"I guess you mean Hy Maxim," said Tony. To his surprise, real interest popped into Pierce's eyes.

"*Hy Maxim!*" he said incredulously. "What's he dong in this?"

"Plenty," said Tony. "He smashed Carl's darkroom, tried to steal library files from my girl's bedroom, and probably tore Satterlee's place to shreds. And he's the man who first went to Hank Rideout with the story of Janet and Lamar's whereabouts."

"Well, well, well," said Pierce, his eyes vanishing as he smiled. "It's nice to learn, Young, that you even know girls *have* bedrooms. Hy Maxim! If that broken-down blackmailer ever came into my office, I'd have him arrested."

"He did," said Condon, "and, oddly enough, in your New York office. Odder still, he had a note from you recommending him for a staff job. Oddest of all, I was there and recognized him."

"Just a moment, gentlemen," said Pierce, his smile vanishing. "You say he had a recommendation from me?"

"That's right," said Tony.

"Impossible!" snorted Pierce. "You say Maxim walked into your office, Tony, with a letter from me? That he's since been stealing information and is wrapped up tight in these killings? And that he gave young Rideout the information that started it all?"

"That's it," said Condon.

Pierce began to laugh, his huge flanks heaving. Tears streamed down his face. "Gentlemen!" he gasped. "You are both fine journalists. Between you, you've unearthed much valuable information. But for real detective work, give me an old-school reporter."

"Cut the stalling!" snapped Condon unhappily. "I've got a warrant in my pocket charging you with two murders."

"Don't be stupid!" said Pierce brusquely. He was

giving his lightning-change moods full play now that he sat in the driver's seat. "You'll have to change the name on that warrant. I fear me you've missed a very vital point."

"What?" snapped the lieutenant.

"You've missed the point that Maxim's recommendation might easily have been forged. You've forgotten that Maxim nearly served a term for forgery when he got into trouble."

"Did you keep that note?" Condon asked Tony.

"I threw it out," said Tony.

"Hell!" Condon swore. Then he grinned, turned to Pierce. "All right, since you seem to be eliminating yourself, who did do it?"

"That," said Pierce, "I intend to find out myself. But if you can locate Maxim and learn who his real accomplice is, you'll have your killer. Remember, the Talbot girl must have been deeply involved."

Tony and the detective exchanged glances. Both of them remembered the elevator boy's description of Connie's supposed lover, realizing that by a wide margin the editor failed to fill the bill. The editor rose unsteadily to his feet.

"I know," he said firmly, "who committed these murders. But I'm going to need proof before I tell you. There's just one thing wrong with the way you've worked this case, gentlemen. You've gone way overboard on motive. Remember that."

With the relaxing of the tension, Tony became aware of a sharp draft on the back of his neck, realized it came from the French windows behind him, turned to see curtains fluttering. Then came a blaze, a crash, a sudden smell of cordite. Then silence.

Both Condon and Tony dropped instinctively to the carpet. But Malin Pierce was slow to follow them. He stood without moving, save for his hands, which pawed with apparent casualness at his vest.

Then his fingers grew suddenly crimson, and he collapsed with an odd sound, half sigh and half whistle, fell forward with a room-shaking thud to lie motionless on his face.

THE PLAINCLOTHESMAN CAME charging into the room just as Condon and Tony were picking themselves up. Malin Pierce was lying motionless, a mountain of inert humanity in the middle of the carpet. The lieutenant, his face white with rage, issued orders as he pulled the revolver from his belt holster.

"Dixon," he snapped at the first of the plainclothesmen, "take care of Pierce here, if there's anything to take care of. O'Toole, you keep that mob outside from getting in here — and put men in position outside to see that none of them get away. Get Mr. Rideout to give you a hand and call the medical examiner. Tony, you come with me."

They raced through the French windows to the balustraded terrace. The rain had stopped, and the dimmed-out silhouettes of the Central Park West skyscrapers were unrelieved by light against the sky.

But nothing stirred between where they stood at the north end of the terrace and the row of potted poplars that marked the southern balustrade some sixty feet away.

"Hell and damnation!" roared Condon. "What an almighty sucker I'm going to look like, letting them get the man I had a warrant for in my pocket."

"Hey!" said Tony. "What's this? Get a load of it."

He stooped to pick up a shapeless something that gleamed faintly white on the darkness of the terrace flagstones. It developed, on closer examination, into a small embroidered linen handkerchief.

"Gardenia," grunted Condon, sniffed it again to be sure. "Yup," he affirmed. "Gardenia. Wait till I find out who had this with them."

"Look's like a girl's," said Tony. "Anyway, now you know that I'm not the guy you're looking for. And you know that Malin Pierce didn't do it."

"It's a hell of a way to prove a man's innocence," said Condon.

He walked to the poplars, made certain there was no chance for anyone to hide behind them or make a getaway over the balustrade at that point.

"Let's go back and see who this belongs to," Condon said, sniffing the handkerchief again and scowling. "How's Pierce?" he asked Dixon when they were back in the lounge.

The plainclothesman shook his head.

"He ain't," he said succinctly. "Dead as a mackerel."

Most of the party folk were huddled together at the east end of the big ballroom. As Condon entered, followed by Tony, a sudden hush fell over the assemblage, broken only by some woman's nervous hiccups.

Rideout was standing apart from the others with Lee, Paul and Janet Saunders. And at the west end of the room was a quivering Leon Satterlee, backed up by a beetle-browed husky sanitarium attendant. In his hand the nervous wreck held his thick glasses, which were apparently shattered beyond repair.

His eyes were unexpectedly small and red-rimmed deprived of their magnifying lenses, and the attendant was clumsily mopping with a bandanna at a small cut over Satterlee's left cheekbone. Tears were streaming down the gossip collector's face.

"What happened in there just now?" Hank Rideout asked the lieutenant in low tones. "I've done what you said. No one's left the apartment."

"Thanks," said Condon. His foot was beating a rapid tattoo on the floor, and he was gnawing his lower lip.

"Was it a shot?" Rideout asked then. "We heard something out here, but it wasn't very loud through the door."

"Yes," said Condon in a flat voice. "It was a shot, all right. Some murdering rat got out on that terrace somehow and listened in on the session. And just when Pierce was getting interesting, this tomato opened a French window and let Pierce have it."

"Good God!" said Rideout, suddenly and palpably affected by the news. "Is he —"

"Yes," said Condon. "He's dead." He didn't wait for this statement to take its inevitable effect. Instead, he turned on Lee. "In the absence of a police matron, and since I can't haul the whole mob in, I want you to take charge of searching the women. Find out if any of them are carrying a gun and learn anything else about them you can. We'll take care of the men while you're doing it."

Quick and efficient search conducted by Hank, Tony and one of the plainclothesmen, under Condon's crisp command, revealed the mixed and curious nature of some of the guests present. Five revolvers and a Colt automatic were turned up on the male side of the gathering.

"Some of these eggs would have made nice house guests for a Cicero jam session in prohibition days," said Tony.

"Don't rub it in," said Hank Rideout.

They finished with their search, and Lee came in from the women's dressing room, where she'd been at work.

"Look what I dug," she said to Condon, handing him a pair of pearl-handled twenty-fives she'd uncovered in as many evening bags. "And I do mean evening bags," she concluded. No offense, Mr. Rideout. But honestly, some of those —"

"Okay, Miss Rankin," said Condon, refusing to be amused. "Stick right here a minute." He looked over the weapons she had found, looked again at those taken from the men, shook his head angrily. "Damn it!" he growled. "None of these things has been fired this evening!"

He was still voicing his displeasure at the unfortunate turn the case had taken when a uniformed policeman arrived via the private elevator and was admitted by the men on guard. He was carrying a black automatic of the conventional mail-order variety. With solicitude for possible fingerprints, he held it wrapped in a handkerchief.

"I picked this up on the sidewalk just a few minutes ago," he said to the lieutenant. "It came within six inches of crowning a guy in an opera hat on the sidewalk. When I picked it up out of the gutter, the barrel was still warm."

Condon grabbed it, handkerchief and all, and sniffed at the muzzle. His nose wrinkled at the aroma of cordite, but the despondency left his tired face.

"This is our baby," he said eagerly. "Officer, I'll remember this in my report."

Condon laid the murder weapon down on a table beside him where he could keep an eye on it.

"Have you a list of your guests, Mr. Rideout?" he asked.

"I can identify all the men," said the young newspaper owner promptly. "But I'm afraid that most of these women are strangers to me. You see, I issue invitations only to men as a rule and trust to their discretion in selecting partners for an affair of this sort. I hope you —"

"I get it," said Condon with a sigh. He cast a jaundiced eye at the females wandering in from the dressing room where they'd been searched by Lee and shook his head.

"I took down their names when I went over them," said Lee unexpectedly, stepping forward and scanning a piece of paper. "I got their addresses too, Lieutenant."

"What makes you think a gang of pigeons like this would give you the right time?" the detective inquired.

Lee winked at him with a wise grin.

"I went through their bags, of course," she said. "Eleven of them had driver's licenses. Fourteen more carried Actor's Equity cards — though I have my doubts about the sort of talents some of them have."

"That girl's terrific," Hank Rideout whispered in Tony's ear.

"She's also fresh," said Tony. "Remind me to paddle her bottom when I get her home."

"I can think of worse disciplinary assignments," said Rideout.

"You'll simply have to take the other five on their face value," Lee went on blandly. "However, they weren't among the gun toters."

"Baby — Miss Rankin," said Condon, beaming. "If you ever want a job on the force, call me up. You're good. Any of them give you any trouble?"

"Just one," she said, putting a finger on the list that the detective now held. "Here — this one."

"Mrs. Tony — hey! What is this?" said the detective. "Mrs. Tony Young. What about her?"

"Yes, what about me?" said Maebell, sweeping up on the detective.

She wore a sapphire velvet evening wrap held tightly about her. The blond-thatched swain followed in her wake. Over his arm was draped what might originally have been the "sensational" scarlet gown. No sign of a skirt showed beneath her wrap.

"This — this woman," she said, her voice shaking with fury, "assualted me and ripped off my clothes in the dressing room. I'm not going to stand for it."

"It looks as if you already have," said Condon giving Tony a swift glance, then turning his attention on Lee. "Well, what happened in there?"

"She refused to take off her dress," said Lee. "So naturally, as I was acting on your authority and it was an emergency, I had to use force."

"Was it necessary to strip her?" Condon inquired.

"Maybe not, Lieutenant," said Lee, dropping her long-lashed eyelids modestly. "But I simply couldn't believe that her figure was real. It looked as if she might be hiding all sorts of things."

"You —!" screamed Maebelle as snorts of laughter rose around her.

She advanced on Lee, who looked demurely frightened, then made a grab at her rival. But the wrap fell open, and she had to make a hasty grab to get it back around her in time.

"Take her home," said Condon to Lavery. "See that neither of you leave town. That will be all, Mrs. Young."

"That," said Maebelle venomously, "is what *you* think." She salved what she could of her pride, making a nose-up exit. Condon looked again at Tony, shook his head, then went grim again.

"Okay," he said. "That's enough. What I just said to those two goes for the rest of you. Mr. Rideout, I want you and Miss Saunders-Pierce-Lamar-Cochrane to stay. You too, Tony, and Miss Rankin — and, oh yes, Mr. Satterlee. You and your keeper."

"How about me?" asked Paul Stanton.

Condon shrugged.

"You can stay if you want to," he said.

As the room was clearing, Lee came over to Tony and slipped an arm through his. She pleaded with him with her eyes, but he refused to look at her. Finally she stepped on his foot, and he gave in. Once he did, he was laughing.

"You *are a* damned undisciplined cat," he said.

"I'm really sorry, Tony, but she put one over on me earlier. It was too good a chance to miss. She won't bother you again."

"You don't know Maebelle, honey," said Tony doubtfully. "After this, she'll be after both our hides."

"Maybe," said the girl enigmatically.

She squeezed his elbow to get his attention on what was happening. Condon was still talking to Hank Rideout.

"We'll hold our session right here if you don't mind," he said, and despite his politeness, it was an order. "The boys from headquarters will be going over the other room for quite a good while yet."

"It's all right," said the young millionaire.

With that disposed of, Condon, crackling with suppressed fury and a vitality he'd managed to tap from a hidden reserve, turned on Leon Satterlee, who quivered at his approach, evidently sensing rather than seeing it, for the nervous wreck was obviously blind without his glasses.

"Officer!" he exploded in quavering tones. "I can't stand this! I simply can't go on this way. I *can't!* Look!" He offered, as if they were precious stones, the shattered remnants of his triple-thick spectacles.

"Some vandal," he went on, "some barbarian — some ruthless Mongol — some Cossack deliberately hit me in the eye with his elbow and broke them."

"And where were you when this happened?" snapped Condon, half angry and half puzzled by the odd little man.

"I was — I was," Satterlee stuttered, his face turning crimson. "I was in —"

"Well, where in hell is that?" asked the detective brutally.

Gasping and fluttering like a fish on a dry bank, Leon Satterlee seized Condon's arm convulsively in his canary-claw fingers and drew him to one side of the room, well away from the ladies. The lieutenant listened with mock patience, lifted his brows and turned on the beefy attendant.

"Do you mean to tell me," he said, shaking his head as if shocked to his heels, "that you let him go in *there* all by himself? Shame on you!"

"Listen, buddy," growled the white-coated attendant. He had the voice of a Russian basso profundo. "Lay off me. There's one thing we learn in this racket — we don't try to stop nature in its course. So when a guy's gotta go, he's gotta go."

"Pipe down!" roared the lieutenant. "I'm not interested in your racket — not right now." He paused, puzzled. Then his eyes came alight with sudden interest. "Where in hell *is* this can?" he asked.

"It's right beside the private elevator," said Satterlee after a strictly in-character wince at the rude appellation used by the lieutenant. "I was — well, if you *must* know, I was in this — er — room, when some man, some Visigoth, some Bolshevik"—his voice rose to a wavering scream — "stuck his filthy elbow right through my spectacles. It's a wonder he didn't blind me permanently. As it is, Officer, I can't see my hand in front of my face without them."

"Then," said Condon thoughtfully, "you *are* blind temporarily."

He spun on his heel, went to the rear hall toward the lavatory where the incident had taken place. A few moments later, those gathered in the big room heard his purposeful footsteps emerge to enter the room where the medical examiner and his staff were still preparing to take Malin Pierce's huge corpse downtown to the morgue.

"I must ask you one more question, Mr. Satterlee," said Condon, returning to face the little man.

The latter's eyebrows went into their dance again, and more tears rolled down his cheeks.

"That's all you police ever do — ask questions. People can be murdered — other people's property destroyed — the fruits of a lifetime of conscientious labor wiped out overnight — and all you *policemen* ever do is stand around and ask questions. All right though" — he sighed deeply as if he were undergoing more than flesh and blood could bear with all the patience of a martyr—"I'll answer you if I can."

"That's the spirit," said Condon. "Now — did this — er — vandal offer you any assistance after the accident? Did he try to help you out of your trouble?"

"I'll have you understand right now," snapped Satterlee, his face suffused with rage and injustice, "that it was no accident! He deliberately put his elbow in my eye. I ask you as a supposedly reasonable human being, Officer, how could he get his elbow into

103

my eye unless it were done on purpose?"

"All right, it wasn't an accident," said Condon with apparently inexhaustible patience. "But *did* the Visigoth offer you any assistance after committing his crime?"

"Well," said Satterlee, cocking his head like a sparrow, "as a matter of fact, he did, though I don't see how you knew about it." He regarded the detective with sudden suspicion. "He tried to wipe the bits of glass from my face. He used a handkerchief which stunk — literally stunk."

"Did it by any chance stink like this?" said Condon, obviously relieved at having gotten something from this human squirrel cage.

Tony, having survived many such sessions through sheer stick-to-itiveness in the past, suffered with him as Condon produced the handkerchief they'd found on the terrace after the murder and waved it under the little man's beaklike nose.

Satterlee drew away from it as if it were warm limburger.

"That — that was *it!*" he said dramatically, held his nose and turned away. "Take it away from me, for God's sake!"

"Is this your handkerchief?" asked Condon, turning to Janet.

She looked at it, saw the initials, nodded.

"Naturally," she said pleasantly. "But where did *you* get it?"

"If you don't know," said the lieutenant, "I'm certainly not going to tell you. Damn it, this *really* makes it tough."

"*Mr.* Condon," said Satterlee, mincing toward the lieutenant's voice and speaking unexpectedly in his shrill, pseudo-cultured tones. "*Would* you be very much put out if *I* should ask *you* a question?"

"Not a bit of it, sweetheart," said Condon brutally.

"I came up here from a sick bed voluntarily," said the nervous wreck, every line in his posture suggesting

104

that he'd been put through the wringer by the Gestapo. "I came here to give you information of my own free will and under no compulsion. So what happens? I am beaten up and cut by an insane bushman, then held a prisoner here against my will and not allowed to talk. Would you *please* tell me what I've done to be subjected to such hideous indignities?"

"Just a minute," said the detective. "If you don't take *all* night about it, will you tell me what you left this bed of pain, *et cetera,* to come here and give us?"

Another long and futile argument ensued. It was not until after a good twenty minutes of senseless bickering that Satterlee finally gave in.

"I came from what may well be my death bed," he said dramatically, "to tell you that no matter how guilty he may look, no matter how seriously he may appear to be involved, Malin Pierce is not guilty of murder. In fact, he's in more danger from the killer of Curtis Lamar and Miss Talbot than he is of going to the electric chair."

"My God!" said the lieutenant, clapping a hand to his forehead. His manner changed, became hammily unctuous. *Mr.* Satterlee," he went on, "I can assure you that on your word and your word alone I shall do my uttermost to have Malin Pierce relieved of all charges against his name. I am afraid"—and Tony was suddenly petrified lest he call the little neurasthenic "darling"—"that there is nothing I can do at the moment."

"You mean he's already in jail?" Satterlee asked with relish. "In that case he'll sue you for false arrest. He'll—"

"I mean," Condon roared with all the power in his voice, "that someone went out on that balcony half an hour ago while I was questioning Pierce in the other room and shot him through the French windows right in front of my eyes. He's dead — murdered, do you understand?"

But the little man was past understanding. He had

fainted, fallen backward into the burly arms of the deep-voiced attendant. Again a trace of foam showed at the corners of his mouth.

"See what you done?" said the attendant belligerently. "My boss ain't going to like this a bit."

"Take him away to wherever you keep him," groaned Condon.

There was a long silence following the exit of the sanatarium couple, a silence which was broken finally by the swish of soda as Condon poured himself a virile highball.

"Now," said the detective, having recovered a portion of his aplomb, "I think you'd better tell me exactly how that handkerchief of yours got out on the terrace, Miss What-ever-your-name-is. Whoever shot Malin Pierce must have left it there. How about it?"

"I may have had reasons for disliking my real father," said the blonde girl quietly, "but patricide is not one of my vices. I really haven't the slightest idea.".

"I think perhaps I can take care of it for you," said Hank Rideout. "Miss Lamar — and by the way, Lieutenant, that's her legal name — had it in her hand while she was sitting beside me on the lounge in the other room. But I'm almost positive she left it there on the sofa when we left the room to give you an opportunity to question Malin Pierce alone. At any rate, she asked me if I'd seen it a moment later."

"And I remember that too," said Lee thoughtfully. "Lieutenant, he's right. She got some make-up in her eye and had to borrow mine to get it out."

"I can back that too," Paul Stanton put in. "I was standing right beside them when that happened."

"Hell!" said Condon bitterly. "That helps — I don't think. What happened in here anyway after you all rejoined the party?"

Everyone looked blank, and the detective put his glass down on a table, managing to avoid an array of coasters put there for the purpose.

"Take it one at a time," he went on as no one answered him. "Miss Lamar, you go first."

"I came out with the other three," she began, and paused, looking thoughtful as she reviewed the proceedings mentally. "Then I got this stuff in my eye and found I'd mislaid my handkerchief.

"After that, I left the others. I wanted to find a play producer Hank had introduced me to earlier, so I cruised around on my own. Then, when the trouble started, Hank rounded me up and took me under his wing again."

"How about you, Miss Rankin?" the detective asked.

"I did more or less the same," said Lee. "I helped Janet get the stuff out of her eye, then went off on my own. I wanted to get a good close-up of somebody here while I had the chance."

"Who?"

"Tony's wife, and she's no song cue," snapped Lee. "I was just maneuvering into position when the trouble started. Paul Stanton came and rounded me up and took me to Mr. Rideout and Janet."

"And you, Stanton?" Condon inquired.

"I was with Rideout for a moment or two after we left you, Lieutenant," said the business manager. "Then I had a drink or two and just drifted around talking to people I knew. I was near Miss Rankin when things began to happen and saw she was alone, so I took her to the others."

"How about you, Rideout?"

"Well, I was the host at this unfortunate affair," said the young millionaire. "I must have spoken to at least twenty persons between leaving the other room and your detective calling me."

"Okay," said the detective. "That'll be all for now. Miss Rankin, I'll drive you and Tony home if you like."

"Thanks," said Tony, exhaling his relief that the session was at last over. "How about it, Lee?"

"I've never ridden in a police car," she said, smiling her acceptance.

"This'll be a taxi," said Condon.

They went to get their wraps, and Hank Rideout pulled Tony aside briefly.

"Get some sleep," he said. "I'll be over at the Bretagne tomorrow until three in the afternoon. This place is too ornate for me to sleep in. But I want those figures of yours before I go back to Philadelphia. Sorry about this evening."

"You couldn't help it, Hank," said Tony. "As a matter of fact, it was anything but a dull party."

Tony shook hands with his host, trying to fit him in as a possible murderer. Then he gave it up. The case was driving him bats.

"See here, Phil," he said in the elevator, "wasn't that kind of a quick going over?"

"I'll say it was," said the detective. "But I'm too tired for the routine. The boys'll take care of that. That lavatory beside the back elevator has a small window opening onto the terrace. It shows signs of having been opened recently. Someone went through it, knocked off Pierce, then came back the same way. Whoever it was probably locked the door so that no one would catch him at it."

"Then you mean the guy who knocked off Satterlee's glasses did it?" Tony asked.

"Yup," said Condon, lighting a cigarette, "unless, as I'm half inclined to believe, Mr. Satterlee went through there himself."

"How about the handkerchief then?"

"Yeah," said Condon, slumping in the cab seat and stretching his legs. "How about it? *You* explain it, and we've got the case all sewed up!"

SEVEN

IT WAS ONLY BECAUSE of the murder of Malin Pierce that Tony got at least half of a sorely needed night's sleep. He and Lee were both so dog-tired that, by mutual consent, he neither asked to come up in the elevator with her nor did she invite him. He kissed her quickly and sleepily, took a quick taxi ride to check out of the hotel and get his things, finally turned in between his own sheets. When the alarm clock woke him up — much too early after what he'd been through — and he got under a shower, he felt moderately well rested.

Arriving early at the office, he forced the last dregs of fatigue from his mind and put all thoughts of the horrendous events of the week-end firmly in the back of his brain. He had a job to do, a big job — the most important of his life — and he was resolved not to muff it.

"If I crash through on this," he told himself grimly, "a lot of amiable dead wood is going to be walking the streets."

This was the least pleasant feature of his program.

Malin Pierce had so overstaffed the outfit that its personnel, in a vain endeavor to make themselves valuable, were cluttering up production.

If he were going to make Phalanx go, he'd have to do it his own way — and he believed in keeping the best only and keeping them occupied.

His Sunday magazine project included a much more even balance between fact and fiction with a women's department that would bring on a Sabbath battle between male and female members of the family to see who got hold of it first.

Contrary to the policy heretofore, he believed in splashing plenty of pretty girls around and using plenty of color — Phalanx had one of the best color presses in the world lying almost idle in the great Philadelphia plant.

He concentrated so hard on his statement of aims and reckoning of costs that he was barely aware that Lee had not come in. Anyway, he told himself in a brief return to consciousness, he didn't need her at the moment, and she was doubtless so worn out by the dreadful week-end that she was sleeping it off.

Carl Martin, as it happened, was late too. It was after ten-thirty in the morning, and Tony had nearly finished his plans when the photographer finally arrived. A roar of rage from the developing room, followed by a loud succession of weird and terrible Spanish oaths, informed him that his picture man had come in.

A moment later, puffing like an outraged sea lion, Martin came storming into Tony's office. His long face a thundercloud of flesh, he slapped both hands down on his boss's desk.

"Listen," he said angrily, talking through his teeth. "Some dirty lousy son got into my studio and ripped up all my plates."

"You don't say so," said Tony mildly, leaning back in his chair. "Have you seen the morning papers, my friend?" He pointed to where they lay on the table with news of Malin Pierce's murder crowding the war news over to the side of the page.

"I'll be damned!" said Martin incredulously, giving them a suspicious run-through to make sure they weren't dummies or some sort of a gag.

"I'll be damned!" he repeated weakly after a moment of silence. "Well, Tony, I guess we'll both be looking for new jobs now."

"Don't give up the ship, Carl," said Tony quietly, lighting a cigarette. "If things break right for us, we're both set pretty."

Carl looked at Tony suspiciously. He started to speak, checked himself, then blurted it out.

"Gosh, Tony," he said, "you didn't kill the old fat fool, did you?"

Tony put back his head and had his first good laugh in days.

"No such luck," he gasped finally. "Not that I haven't wanted to often enough. He's been in my hair since the first day I came on this job. By the way, Carl, look through those scandal sheets and see if my name's in there anywhere."

With this, he turned his full attention back to his work. He got through it in twenty minutes, spent another ten checking it over. It conveyed, he decided, just about what he wanted it to. When he looked up, Carl was still immersed in the papers.

"How about it, Carl?" Tony asked. "Have they smeared us much?"

"Uh uh," said the photographer, shaking his head. "You ain't in here, boss. Why — did you hold him while somebody else gave it to him or something?"

"I was there at the party," said Tony. "In fact, I was in the room with him when he was shot." He paused as sudden inspiration seized him. "Did you ever know a long drink of water by the name of Hy Maxim?"

"Sure," said Carl Martin. "He was a reporter. He was also a rat and louse of the first water. What about him?" His black eyebrows rose in inquiry.

"He," said Tony deliberately, "is the tomato who broke into your studio. He was there all the time I was talking to Hank Rideout in here yesterday afternoon, but he got away before we knew he was around."

"So," said the photographer musingly, "he's in on these killings too."

Tony looked up sharply.

"What makes you think so?" he asked.

"The pictures," said Carl. "The pictures you had me take of the first stiff."

"My God, Carl!" said Tony, really alarmed. "Were they in there? I thought you took them with you when you left Saturday."

"Naw," said the cameraman with a reassuring leer. "I burned them and sprinkled the ashes on the Empire State building from a Mitchell Field P-Forty. If you think I left them around here, you ain't giving me credit for the few brains God gave me. But the fact that that louse Maxim was on the prowl for them ties him up with the killings for my two bucks."

He had edged over toward Tony, now craned his neck to get a solid squint at what the latter was working on. Apparently he got the drift of it, for his eyes narrowed.

"Hey!" he said. "You said Rideout was here talking with you yesterday — and you were up at his place when Pierce was shot. Are *you* going to take over?"

"Don't speak ill of the dead," Tony chided. He put his finger to his lips, looked around with elaborate cautiousness. "Keep it out of the papers, will you? It's not in the bag yet. So keep your fingers crossed."

"I'm with you, kid," said Carl. "You'll do good."

"What makes you think so?" said Tony curiously.

"You got class, kid, and you know what it's all about," was the unexpected reply.

"Why, thank you, Carl," said Tony. "I didn't know you cared."

"*Braaaack!*" The photographer gave him the bird

he merited. Then his saturnine face grew serious. "But that's not going to stop me from running down that rat who busted up my files. I'll murder him!" He rubbed his permanently fluid-stained hands together in anticipation that was at once sanguine and sanguinary.

"Just find him," said Tony. "That's all I want."

"You mean —" Carl looked thoroughly astonished. "Can I go off on the prowl now, chief? You ain't got no assignments for me or nothing?"

"Just one," said Tony quietly. "Go after Maxim and find him, and when you do, call in before you take it out of his hide. If I'm not here, Lee will be."

"How come you're interested?" Carl asked, puzzled. "He hasn't done much *real* damage — just given me a big headache."

"You aren't the only one who's after him," said Tony. "I'd like to get my hands on him myself. So would the whole damned police department. You hit the nail on the thumb when you said he was tied up in these killings."

"Okay, I'll call you," said Carl, smiling slowly and not pleasantly. "If the punk's in the city, Ill dig him, don't worry." He stalked out, rubbing the knuckles of his right hand into the palm of his left.

Tony sat back, thinking he'd had a good solid hunch. Martin, an ex-crime photographer, was a very able bloodhound. He knew the ropes from Bowery flophouse owners to the head waiter at the Stork Club, could draw blood from turnips who wouldn't talk to a detective or harness bull on principle.

He decided he'd better call Condon and inform him that he'd set the cameraman on Maxim's trail with blood in his eye. But before he could pick up the telephone, it commenced to ring. Philadelphia was calling.

The main office, deprived of its fountain of being by the murder of Malin Pierce, was a madhouse. Bartels, Pierce's managing editor, shot a barrage of questions at him. What about the dog story? What about the fireboat angle on the arson and sabotage yarn? What about pictures for the night club and taxi dance hostess expose? The cover for the issue after next?

"Hold your water!" said Tony, overwhelmed by the barrage of questions. "Why in hell pour all this on me? Only the fireboat and taxi dance stuff was supposed to come through this office."

"Because Hank Rideout just called the office and said you were running the works."

For a moment Tony couldn't speak. Rideout certainly moved fast when his mind was made up.

"Things are still waist deep in muck up here," Tony finally told Bartels. "And I'm still mucked up in them. I'll do the best I can to keep the routine stuff moving at this end. And I'll get down to the main office tomorrow — today, if possible."

"Okay, Tony," said Bartels. "By the way, congratulations."

"Thanks," said Tony, hanging up. He thought then about the fact that neither of them had mentioned M. P., wondered if authority would make him as universally disliked.

Lee came in then, took off her hat, and shook out her long bob before coming over to kiss him.

"Hey," he told her breathlessly when they came out of it. "Guess what — I've just been informed from Philadelphia that I'm the new executive editor of Phalanx. How do you like that?"

She began to get excited too, gave him a darting kiss that missed his mouth and put lipstick on his chin Before she could do further damage, the telephone rang again. This time it was Condon.

"What's on your mind?" Tony inquired.

"How about giving me a pat on the back for keeping you and your girl friend out of the papers?"

"I'll buy the drinks," said Tony, "but that's no event. That's routine. The drinks are always on me when you're around." He went on to tell the detective of his hunch and sending Carl Martin out to look for Hy Maxim.

"I hope he's lucky," said the detective doubtfully. "*We* haven't been so far. If he does find him, get hold of me at once through headquarters. I'll keep them posted on where I can be reached. That fellow's dangerous."

"How about Satterlee?" asked Tony. "Has he talked?"

The detective's reply was profane. "He's turned on his nervous breakdown again," he said bitterly. "Even the boys at the sanatarium seem to think it's on the level. They won't let me see him."

Tony laughed and hung up. Then he gathered his material for Rideout together, put it in a manila envelope.

"Honey," he told Lee, "hold down that switchboard while I'm at the Bretagne seeing Rideout. Here's what they're running in circles about in Philly." He gave her the list of assignments and went on his way.

The horrors of the forty-eight hours just past faded out before the sharp exultation brought on by his sudden promotion. He knew it meant work, repsonsibility — the sort that would make or break him for keeps — but it was the chance he'd been waiting for.

RIDEOUT, FULLY DRESSED, was breakfasting from a handsome platter of kidneys and bacon in the living room of his suite when Tony arrived. He answered the door himself, his mouth full of food, motioned him to a chair while he washed down his food with coffee.

"Congratulations, Tony," he said. "You're a hundred-to-one long shot, but so far my long shots have done more for me than any so-called 'logical' choices" — he rapped on the wood of the chair he sat in — "and I do mean so far."

"Bartels caught me off guard just now," said Tony.

"I was still buried in this prospectus of mine. I told him to carry on as best he could until I could get down there to take over. Meanwhile, here's the stuff I promised you last night."

He tossed the manila envelope onto the tablecloth in front of the young millionaire, went back to his chair and lit a cigarette.

It took Hank Rideout a solid hour to finish studying the typed matter Tony had prepared. He went over some details three and four times, made frequent notes on a pad of paper at his elbow, asked occasional keen questions. Finally he put the papers back into the envelope, balanced it thoughtfully in his hand.

"Do you mind if I keep this?" he asked.

"Hell!" said Tony, hoping his voice didn't sound as jumpy as it felt in his throat. "I could write it again in my sleep. It's stuff I've been thinking over and dreaming about for years. Probably looks pretty silly in the cold light of dawn."

"Do you really think so?" Rideout asked sharply.

"No," said Tony, "but plenty of my suggestions are radical, to put it mildly. However, that's the way I see the outfit making a profit. It means spending more money, you know."

"That," said Hank Rideout quietly, "is up to you. I've already sunk so much in what has begun to look like a bottomless funnel that I can't afford not to take chances.

"Remember, I didn't put you into this job merely because you broke my nose in a football game. Take a look at these." He pushed a trio of letters across the table to where Tony could reach them. "I've quite naturally been checking up on Paul."

Tony's eyebrows rose as he scanned them. They were a revelation, and not a pleasant one. Paul Stanton's last sales trip had been far from the triumphal progress he'd reported so jubilantly two days before.

True enough — the supplement had been sold to a number of important key newspapers throughout the

Middle West. But in each case it had been sold on the dubious condition that it met with public approval within a month of purchase — in other words, Phalanx was committed on the slimmest sort of trial basis. More serious, Boston, which was already carrying the supplement, showed definite symptoms of wanting to sever connections as soon as possible.

"It's evident from these letters," said Rideout dryly, "that things haven't been going as well anywhere as I had been led to believe. And this mess up in Boston shows us how the wind lies. It's my guess the others were willing to give us a trial because of Boston. You've got to do a super reclamation job in an impossibly short time. Do you think you can handle it?"

Tony pondered the question. Knowing Paul, he could understand the enthusiasm and optimism that had run away with him and led him into overreaching himself. Those were the qualities that made him the fine salesman and promoter he was. But, combined with Malin Pierce's wretched editorial achievement, these same qualities had put the entire outfit into quicksand.

"You'll have to have your Philadelphia boys get out some S.O.S. promotion," he said quietly, feeling his plan grow more solid with each passing moment. "And it can't be on this Sunday's issue, because we can't save it now. It's already pretty well through the works, and any replacements we have would only be worse — though the issue is going to be a stinker."

"Then what are the boys going to promote?" asked Rideout curiously,

"They'll have their material tomorrow," Tony said. "If it weren't for this stinking mess we're all in here, I might be able to get some of it to them by this evening. But they can follow the outline of policy I just gave you and dig stuff out of that."

"Okay," said Rideout, noting it down on his pad. "Can you be any more specific?"

"No," said Tony. "Not now. As long as they suggest a 'Comes the revolution' with a vast improvement in Phalanx along the lines I've precised this morning. The idea is to keep the papers we have hanging on out of curiosity for a few more days. Their job is in the nature of a delaying action. It's a sideline at best."

"How do you figure that, Tony?" asked Hank Rideout. "The promotion seems pretty damned important to me."

"It is, of course," said Tony, his face beginning to light up with enthusiasm. "But our main promotion will be in the new sheet itself. If I have to keep the whole gang working every night between now and Friday, I'm going to get out a make-up of the magazine for a week from this Sunday in time to reach the member newspapers of this syndicate before Pierce's last hash job gets to them."

"I hear you," said Rideout. He smiled slowly, becoming caught in the mesh of Tony's enthusiasm. "I think we're going to get along. But how do you propose to do it?"

"By busting wide open and getting it out," said Tony. "It won't be an ideal job — it can't be. And it's going to cost money under present conditions. We won't have time to shop around."

"I told you money's no object," said Rideout. "I meant it. What are you going to do?"

"I'm going to start today — calling agents, finding the stories and lead articles we need. I have a woman for the distaff side — Daisy Cornet, the old *Vogue* and *Harper's Bazaar* girl. She's a swell name, and she's aching to get back into it. M. P. couldn't see her. We'll have to top magazine prices to get the literary agents to call good stories in and let us have them."

"Yes, Tony," said Rideout, "we're going to get along."

They talked for another hour on technical matters, and at the end of that time the young publisher seemed to have almost as complete a grasp on the problems to be faced as had Tony himself.

118

"We'd better get the ball rolling right now. I'll leave for Philadelphia on the two o'clock train and you follow as soon as the police let you. I believe we've really got a chance."

He reached for the telephone, called Bartels, and he and Tony took turns talking to the man in charge at the home office, who was bewildered but anxious to do his best. It was in the midst of this lengthy series of instructions that the operator's voice cut in. Lee's voice came through.

"Tony," she said. "I hate like hell to bother you now, but Carl just called up. He says he's got Hy Maxim located, and says he can't hold him much longer unless you get up there in a hurry. I've had the devil's own time getting you."

"It's okay," said Tony, giving Hank Rideout a nod. "Where is he hiding out?"

"Carl says to meet him on the northwest corner of Columbus Avenue and Eighty-third," said Lee carefully. "And, Tony, for God's sake be careful, will you? I'm scared."

"Take it easy, honey, and don't worry," he told her. "I'm practically on my way now."

He hung up, turned to Hank Rideout, who was showing evidences of curiosity.

"Was that *the* Rankin?" he asked. "She was marvelous last night."

"It was," said Tony, "and she's still marvelous. But I'm going to have to break this up. My photographer, Carl Martin, has just located the missing Hy Maxim. I've got to get up there right away. Can you carry on?"

"I can carry on," said the young millionaire. "And if finding Maxim and digging out what he knows gets this murder thing off all of our necks, it's worth it. We need you in Philly this minute. Is there anything I can do for you?"

"As a matter of fact, there is," said Tony. "You might call up Condon at headquarters and tell him

I'm going to the northwest corner of Columbus Avenue and Eighty-third Street to see our friend." He rose and reached for his hat and coat.

Tony's taxi seemed to be suffering from a serious attack of inertia. Every slow bus or truck seemed to settle down in front of it and preclude all chance of passing.

He blued the air with curses as a horse-drawn delivery cart slowed it down to a walk under the last surviving elevated in Manhattan for a full three blocks. He pulled a couple of dollars from his pocket, tossed them to the driver as they were finally halted and jammed inextricably in a tangle of traffic half a block from the destination. He covered the rest of the distance on foot at a dead run.

His destination proved to be an extremely ordinary red brick structure, four stories high, with a little magazine and candy store on the ground floor and dingily curtained rooms lurking behind dusty windows above it. A quick look convinced him that neither Carl nor Hy Maxim was in the tiny store, so he found the entrance to the rooms and went in.

For a moment he heard nothing. Then, from almost directly overhead, came a loud crash, which was followed directly by the thud of a body colliding with something violently and a muffled crash. He took the stairs three at a time.

As he reached the second floor landing, a door across the narrow corridor burst open almost in his face. A figure came staggering out backward, tripped over the rim of the linoleum carpet and fell flat on its back. His mouth looked as if it had been through a meat grinder, and his lower face was streaming with blood.

Another figure appeared in the doorway, a tall, lanky figure that gathered itself for a vicious spring at the fallen man. But Tony, moving on reflex action alone, was too quick for the pursuer. He charged in, his legs driving, butted the erstwhile reporter full in his flat stomach. His charge didn't topple Maxim, who seemed to be surprisingly tough, but it sent him reeling back into the room with Tony stumbling after him.

Tony didn't have time to look around for a weapon. By the time he'd recovered his balance sufficiently to lift his head and see what was going on, Maxim had seized a whiskey bottle from the mantel and knocked off the neck on the rim of the dirty marble. The liquor was spurting out as he moved forward, jabbing with the jagged edge at Tony's face.

SOMEHOW TONY MANAGED to twist himself out of the path of Hy Maxim's first furious assault. The latter slammed past him so hard he crashed the wall, and Tony had an opportunity to swing a real rabbit punch to the ex-reporter's cervical vertebrae. But as he pivoted, he caught an ankle in the rungs of an overturned chair and went down, sprawling.

He managed to shake his foot loose while on his way down, doubled his knees, and blasted the worrisome piece of furniture at Maxim, who was coming for him again. It brought the ex-reporter to his knees with a curse and caused him to send the broken bottle flying as he flung both hands forward to break his fall.

But Maxim, it quickly developed, was unexpectedly quick as well as tough. He bounced to his feet and right into Tony before the newly appointed executive could get up. He lifted his arms to ward off the blows, but a hard right fist came over his guard and crashed off the point of his jaw, sending him reeling back all the way across the room to the other wall, where he smashed through a picture frame with his elbow.

He feinted with his left, got up on the balls of his feet and threw a right-hand punch at Maxim, hitting him high on the cheekbone. The blow bounced off as if a baby had struck it, leaving no mark on the ex-reporter's flesh and no visible effect on his attack. Yes, Maxim could certainly handle himself.

A tatto of blows to the stomach, abdomen and diaphragm made Tony suddenly violently ill. He doubled up, tried to throw a football block at his tormentor, but another right to the button straightened him, and he knew he couldn't. The room was whirling crazily about him.

He swung a couple of punches, saw the sneer on Maxim's face as they missed by too many inches. He had to do something. He tried to kick the ex-reporter, but his feet were held to the floor by leaden weights. He was done then, and he knew it and stood there, helpless, waiting for the knockout punch to land. Maxim, disdaining defense now, drew back his right hand, cocked it, got set to deliver the crusher.

Again Tony didn't feel it. He'd unconsciously closed his eyes, opened them again to see if he were lying on the floor. But he was still upright after a fashion, though the room around him behaved like an airplane doing all-out stunts and Maxim was still in front of him, still sneering, his fist still cocked. He seemed to move like a man in a slow-motion movie camera. Then he began to dwindle, getting shorter and shorter as if he were turning into a dwarf.

"That's very funny — very funny indeed," thought Tony, trying to work it out in his paralyzed brain. He turned his eyes down, saw that Maxim's knees were buckling. He wondered when he'd landed the blow that had done that to this superman.

All at once Maxim lurched, fell over sideways, revealing a bloody-faced Carl Martin crouched behind him, the now empty broken bottle clenched in his uplifted right fist, ready to be swung again. It came down squarely atop Maxim's head, where it broke with a curious popping sound and shivered to the floor in fragments.

"Gosh!" said Tony, making a grab for the wall behind him and barely getting it. "He was an awful tough apple, wasn't he?"

At that moment, Condon came running into the room at the head of a quartet of policemen. Tony tried to grin, lifted a hand from the supporting wall in salute. Everything, room, Condon, Carl and cops, went blurry then, whirled into a funnel of blackness in which filaments of light faded slowly away as he fainted and fell to the floor.

The next thing he knew, or rather felt, was something that burned in his throat, made him bubble and gag and cough.

"That's better," said a voice he thought somehow he ought to know from somewhere. It was a policeman's voice, or so his aching head told him. What was the guy's name — not that he really gave a good damn, but it offered something to think about beyond the agony inside his skull.

He opened his eyes, got a blurred impression of people bending over him. Condon and Carl Martin, bloody mouth and all, were there, and they looked as worried as if they were minding a sick baby.

"Help me up, you big lugs," he said, and his voice seemed to come from outside on the fire escape. "I'm okay."

Relieved, they lifted him gently and put him into a chair. He was glad it wasn't the bed, because if he lay down again, he feared he'd pass out. His head wasn't ready yet to stand much tipping. He took the bottle from Condon with surprisingly weak hands and drank from it. The liquor brought a stir of life back to his veins, and he began to feel better — not much, but some.

The room stopped doing tricks around him then, and he got a good look at it. Chairs lay broken on the floor, curtains had been dragged down, pictures smashed and knocked to the floor, a table overturned. A couple of policemen stood in the hall doorway, and a couple more stood with a man who, by his black bag and stethoscope, was evidently a doctor, over the prone heap of torn clothes that was the one-time newspaperman Hy Maxim.

"Tony'sh all right," said Martin to the lieutenant.

"If he can take a thlug like that thtraight, he'th okay. Here, Tony, give me that bottle. I took a pathting from that thon of a bith too."

Tony blinked at Carl incredulously as he took the bottle. The usually hard-boiled photographer sounded like something that isn't talked about in what is laughingly called polite society. Condon, after an anxious look at Tony's eyes to see if her were fully conscious, turned his attention to the doctor attending Maxim.

"How about him?" he asked.

The physician looked up and around at him over a pair of gold-rimmed spectacles far down on his nose. He compressed his lips and shook his head.

"He'll be lucky if he lives," he said. "He's got a multiple fracture of the cranium. It's a pip."

"I hope he's unlucky," said the lieutenant in hard tones. "What I really want to know is when in hell he'll be able to do some talking."

"With his concussion?" said the doctor, astonishment in his eyes and voice at the stupidity of such a question. "Maybe in a week if he lasts that long."

"Hell!" Condon swore heartily. "That's my luck in this case. By the way," he asked Martin, "how did you manage to run the son of a louse to earth?"

"Thimple," lisped Carl. He paused to turn away and spit blood on the floor. There was a hideous black void where, until a few minutes before, his front teeth had proudly rested. "I have a friend down at Ninety Shursh Thtreet in Army Intelligenth.

"Every newthpaper bum in town hath applied there for a job thinth the war thtarted. Tho I figured that if thomebody there didn't have hith addreth, he wouldn't be in town. They had it, and my friend gave it to me, and that wath that. I came up here, and he wath in."

"I'll be damned!" said Condon. He looked chagrined, then shook his head and smiled. "By the way, I presume it was self-defense if he doesn't come out of it."

"How about just letting us be written in the book as unidentified assailants?" said Tony.

Condon gave him a look, then shrugged and smiled. "We'll see what we can do," he said.

The doctor, finally finished with wrapping a cocoon of bandages around the ex-reporter's damaged noggin, stood up and came over to where Tony was sitting. After a quick examination, he shook his head.

"You need medical attention yourself, young man. Better get to a hospital for observation right away," he said.

"Hey!" called Carl. "What about me?"

"I am not a dentist," said the physician, going to work on Tony.

Disinfectant, salve, gauze, and a few inches of tape made him feel a bit more in one piece, though his head still felt like a battle ground, and there was a painful catch in his chest when he took a deep breath.

In the meantime, Condon was going through the unconscious Hy Maxim's pockets. A miscelany of objects — pencils, cards, odd bits of paper, unpaid bills and contraceptives — rewarded his search. It was the usual impedimenta of the wandering male. Then he got to the ex-reporter's thick wallet — and whistled. It contained a thick wad of bills — they came to eleven hundred dollars in all — and a single small key, hidden in a tear in the lining.

"Bowery Savings," the lieutenant remarked, squinting at it. "I made a study of these things once. It's a vault key. Doc, you stay here until the ambulance comes and see that Maxim gets to Bellevue in one piece. Feel up to making a trip downtown, Tony?"

"He should be in Bellevue too," said the doctor disapprovingly.

Tony got up slowly, found he could stand, shook his head.

"Nuts!" he said. "I'm coming along with you, Phil."

"Me too?" Carl asked eagerly.

"For God's sake, get to a dentist," said Tony. "Tell

him to send the bill to Phalanx. I'll go crazy if I have to listen to you talking like a nance much longer."

They went downstairs, pushing through a small crowd which had gathered with the arrival of the police. Condon led Tony to a prowl car, squeezed in beside him.

"Bowery Savings, Blank Branch," he told the uniformed driver.

The green-and-white job, siren growling in its upward crescendo, took off with a roar of power, splitting the traffic.

Fifteen minutes later they were far downtown, being ushered into the gleaming brass-and-steel interior of the savings vault. An attendant brought them Maxim's deposit box, put it on a table. It was a large metal case, a couple of feet long, crammed with cards, papers, documents and letters.

Leon Satterlee's files on Curtis Lamar, Malin Pierce, Janet Lamar and the Rideouts took up most of the space, along with a few yellowed clippings from old newspapers relating to the story. They were both voluminous and amazingly complete.

Apparently Satterlee had known for years that Lamar was not dead, that he had been living two floors above him at the Van Dyke, a victim of agoraphobia. On what had been evidently the outer folder of the Lamar file was scrawled, *Look for trouble here.*

And at the very bottom of the box, beneath all the files and other items, was a single letter, typewritten, undated, unsigned.

My dear Maxim:

To say that your proposition interests me is putting it mildly. I am fully aware of your more than doubtful record, but the matter is of such immediate and vital importance to me that I am inclined to believe that something like the action you suggest must be undertaken promptly. I do not think your approach is the soundest available.

There is an indirect method which is at least as certain and at least twice as safe. I feel it would be far better to approach Rideout directly. If handled correctly, he will be certain to carry it to the party we desire to reach. Whether he handles it in person, which I feel sure he will not do, or relays it, does not matter. It is almost bound to have rapid effect.

Needless to say, you will be treated most liberally by me for your suggestions and aid in carrying out this plan. I will deliver to you $1,000 upon completion of the contact and another $4,000 when the affair is consummated. I shall also deliver to you the yearly provision you demand throughout the rest of your life — if the affair goes through as planned, I will hardly be in a position to refuse any reasonable demands on your part.

I will be forced to rely on your discretion, as you must rely on mine, so we are mutually protected. I will even see to your employment if you so desire.

The man who will make the job pay for both of us is Young, now in charge of the New York office. I shall work in his behalf and put in a real boost for him when things blow wide open.

"Well," said Tony, as he and the lieutenant exchanged glances, "where does this get us?"

"Don't ask me," said the detective wearily. "It means only one thing to me — that Pierce was right when he said we were a million miles away on motive. And he proved that already by getting himself shot. And speaking of shot, Tony, you look it."

EIGHT

TONY FELT SHOT. THE vault was beginning to do ground loops around him as had Hy Maxim's rented room a short while before. Instinctively, his hand groped for the nearest wall and sorely needed support.

"I guess I'm all in, Phil," he said.

"Come on," said Condon, taking his arm. "You've got to take it easy for a while. Where to?"

"Perhaps you'd better take me to the office," said Tony slowly. Words came with difficulty. "Lee will know what to do."

Wasting no more time on words, the lieutenant, who had already ordered the contents of Maxim's deposit box held for him and stuffed the letter in his pocket, took hold of Tony's arm and hustled him outside and into a taxicab.

Lee was horrified when she saw him. His face was deadly pale where it wasn't purple from the marks of Hy Maxim's tough fists, and he could barely keep his feet under him. She jammed on her excuse for a hat and mothered him back into a cab.

"What happened to him?" she asked the detective.

"Maxim turned out to be pretty tough," said Condon. "He took a pretty bad beating. What he needs most of all is to lie down. He's had a rough time. Can you handle him, kid?"

"If I can't," said the girl, her lips set in a firm line, "I don't deserve him. I'm going to put him to bed in my place where I can get at him."

Condon rode uptown with them, helped the girl fold him up.

"No hospitals," Tony murmured. "Thanks, honey." His eyes closed, his breathing was deep and regular.

"Why did you let this happen to him?" the girl asked, turning on Condon angrily.

He opened his hands.

"We got there right behind him," he said. "If he'd had sense enough to wait, it would have been all right. But Carl Martin was taking a beating when he got there, so I guess he thought he'd better mix in."

"Carl?" she said, frowning. "What is this Maxim — Superman?"

"He gave a pretty fair imitation," said Condon. "He used to be in the ring. Let Tony sleep. It's the best thing for him. And have a doctor give him a check when he wakes up."

"Don't worry — I will," said the girl. "Damn it! I've got to get back to the office and clean things up. This would happen when all kinds of hell are popping in Philly."

"That's the way things go," said Condon. "I've got to get back downtown."

"Thanks," said Lee. "I didn't mean to blow up. But I love that big baboon for my sins."

"He's a pretty swell guy," said the detective, "but don't tell him I told you. See you later."

When he awoke, Tony felt funny lying in Lee's bed — funny and almost comfortable as long as he didn't turn his head quickly, and entirely content. He remembered what had happened, decided he'd had to go through a hell of a lot to wind up in this particular bed — even alone. He also decided it was worth it.

The room was entirely feminine, with everything brightly draped and cushions kicking around here and there. A pile of wacky French dolls, tossed in a heap on the bureau to make room for him on the bed, stared back at him inanely, especially one of them which had landed upside down with its pom-pommed feet around its frizzly head.

Lee, he decided, would be at the office. Well, there was only one thing to do — wait for her. And he wouldn't mind doing that. He hoped he'd be in condition to make it worth while. Hell, he was the new boss of Phalanx. He had to get moving or else he'd be the boss of nothing within a couple of weeks.

And then something began to ring — ring and ring and his eardrums set up an echo that made his skull scream. He picked up the telephone by the bed optimistically, was greeted with a buzzing dial tone. And the ringing continued.

It had to be the door — and by its insistence it was urgent. He groaned at the thought of getting up, but anything was better than the terrible noise. It could be Condon with urgent news, he decided — or, and even more urgent, Hank Rideout.

Stifling a groan at the agonizing way in which his brains rattled when he tried to move, he felt around on the carpet for his shoes. At which point he discovered he was wearing no clothes. Worse, there were no clothes in sight. He swore without much emotion, wondered what to do.

He finally found a robe. It was a bright blue and yellow terry cloth adorned with playful white dolphins. He got into it with considerable difficulty, had to hunch his shoulders to keep from bursting it open at the back.

"Shut up! I'm coming," he muttered as he moved toward the front door, a ridiculous figure with his hirsute bare shanks. He finally made it, opened it.

Paul Stanton stood there, clucking his tongue as he took in the outfit.

"Holy Moses!" said the manager. "You look like a cross between a lily of the valley and a punchdrunk pug. By the way, I'd like to offer my congratulations."

"Thanks," said Tony.

Paul came on in, so he shut the door and followed him into the living room. He felt a bit more normal, though he was as sore from head to heels as if he'd taken a massage from a mallet. Anyway, he had to see Paul about the new setup at Phalanx.

"How did you know I was here?" he asked, tugging at the cuffs of his robe in a vain effort to pull them down over his forearms. Paul chuckled, sat down, and pulled the inevitable cigar from his breast pocket.

"Your girl told me," he said, chuckling. "Boy, you really are a sight for sore eyes. Have you looked in any good mirrors lately?"

"I haven't dared," Tony said, plopping in another chair. Fortunately, there were cigarettes on the stand beside it so he didn't have to get up again. "As a matter of fact, in spite of appearances, I haven't moved in yet. Not that I wouldn't like to. By the way, we've got plenty to talk about."

"I'll say," said Stanton, going through the ridiculous Sir Basil Zaharoff trick lighting process. "Well, kid. How does it feel to be the works?"

"So far, I've been taking a beating," said Tony. "Otherwise, I like."

"What are your plans for the sheet?" Stanton asked him then, exhaling a series of perfect rings.

"I'm going to save your neck," said Tony. "I'll have dummies of the new set-up in all your cities by Saturday or bust a gut trying. And we'll be on the stands the Sunday after next."

Paul blew out smoke in a quick gust, sighed with relief.

"Boy," he said. "That's the best news I've heard since Phalanx started. I don't mind telling you now that I've had the devil's own time holding onto the ground we've gained while we been selling the mess Pierce was putting out.

"Every paper with a Sunday edition wants a damned good supplement," he went on with an airy wave of his cigar. "It means prestige, increased circulation — shekels. And that's the only language these monkeys understand. What they don't want is an out-of-date section that will drive readers away. If Pierce had only stuck to the original idea — "

"What *was* the original idea?" asked Tony. "By the time I joined the outfit, it was thoroughly buried."

"You're telling me!" said Paul. "We were going to take the old Hearst formula and bring it up to date — sex, treasure, religion. Hell, you know it — but we couldn't get old M. P. to take off his long red flannel underwear.

"But you can do it, Tony. And think of those profits when it gets really clicking. We ought to gross a quarter of a million a week — two-thirds of it net profit!"

"You've got a shock coming," said Tony quietly. "I'm moving in another direction. I know the blind spot you ad men who worked for Hearst have, and I know why you have it — it's made a lot of money in the past. But I've been around long enough to know it won't work any more.

"I'm going to give them plenty they'll want to read," he continued, forgetting his injuries in his interest. "They'll have sex and buried treasure, all right. But I'm going further — give them decent printing, four-color work, name authors, a load of woman's interest, first class fiction — "

"You can't make enough profit that way," said Paul, his face growing hard. "The formula's proved."

"Mine hasn't been proved," said Tony, "but it will be. Hold your water until you see the dummy."

"Hold on," said Paul, rising and pacing the carpet. "Have you talked to Rideout about this?"

"Certainly," said Tony. "He's giving me a free

hand. He's with me. How do you think I got the job?"

"How do I think you got it?" said Paul, standing still. "I *know* how you got it. I've been doing spade work for you for two months."

Tony rose, then stooped a trifle to stamp out his cigarette. He fought to make his motions casual, hoped his pounding heart wasn't audible across the room. At that moment he knew he was face to face with the triple killer of Curtis Lamar, Connie Talbot and Malin Pierce!

If his nerves — badly jangled anyway — hadn't betrayed him, Tony might have gotten away with it. But he jabbed the ashtray a trifle too hard, sent it spinning off the stand to scatter its contents over the rug. Painfully he crouched to pick up the debris. And when he looked up, Paul, his hands in his pockets, was smiling at him oddly.

"So you know," he said quietly, his right fist emerging wrapped around the grip of an automatic.

"Yes, I know," said Tony, a bit too stunned to be frightened. "How did you know I knew?"

"I read the papers," said Paul. "The early afternoon editions carried the story of your and Martin's scrap with Maxim. He had my letter, and I knew that if you'd seen it you'd react when I said what I just did."

Tony felt suddenly weak again, sagged back into the chair.

"You're smart, Paul," he said. "Probably a little too smart."

"You may be right about that," said Paul. "But it's not going to help you. You're the guy — you must be — who framed that suicide at the Van Dyke and threw my train off the track in the first place. You shouldn't have done it, kid. Because, the way things have turned out, I've got to kill you for it."

Tony lit another cigarette. To his surprise, his fingers were steady. This situation was entirely ridiculous — sitting here in Lee's apartment, talking to Paul who was almost his friend. And Paul was going to kill him. It didn't make sense.

But the bodies of Lamar and Connie Talbot and Malin Pierce had been terribly real — they weren't ridiculous. Neither was the dull-finished black muzzle that was pointed at the center of his chest.

Paul could shoot, and shoot well, that was certain. He'd left triple proof behind him in the trail of corpses his ambition had fostered. Tony took a deep drag on his cigarette, looked up at him, took a deep breath. His chest still hurt.

"You'd better make it snappy," he said, wondering why his mind and voice and muscles functioned at all at such a moment. If you don't, Lee may walk in, or maybe Phil Condon."

"I was just thinking of that," said Paul, his tone still entirely amiable. Apparently he took his murders pretty calmly. Hate had nothing to do with it. He was the perfect cold-blooded killer, destroying systematically anything or anyone who got in his path.

"Get up," said Paul slowly, and Tony could see in his eyes that he'd figured out how he was going to do it.

He obeyed. He hadn't much choice in the matter. He was too far from the murderer to make a dive for him, and in too weak condition to put up much of a fight if he did.

"Go into the bathroom," Paul went on, not raising his voice. "And don't try anything. I won't be close enough for you to get at me in time. And I can put a bullet where it won't be easy for you."

"I know that," said Tony, a vivid picture of the killer's accuracy in the other murders rising before his eyes. He shuddered a little, had to fight hard for self-control.

When he reached the white-tiled chamber, he hesitated, tensed the muscles of his back waiting for the slug to tear into his flesh. It would make a hell of a

134

noise in here, he thought. But evidently Paul had thought of that too.

"Take a towel," he said calmly. "Not a face towel, a bath towel — there on the rack."

Tony obeyed and began to get the drift of Paul's plan. He was going to use the towel to muffle the sound of the shot. Why couldn't he toss it into Paul's face and make a fight of it? No, by the time it would take both a towel and himself to cover twelve feet, Paul would be blazing away at him. He was shaking now, as shock left him, desperately frightened and casting for straws to save his life. Hell, he didn't want to die. He had Lee and a terrific job to live for.

"Turn around and face me," Paul went on. "Now toss it to me — low."

He threw it, knee high. Paul caught it in his left hand without letting his gun lose its mark for a moment.

"Okay now, kid," said Paul. "Step forward two paces and stand still. It won't hurt. And don't try to duck behind those doors and lock me out."

He retreated as Tony moved out into the bedroom. The French dolls were still staring at him wide-eyed, even the upside down one. Paul flipped the towel expertly around the barrel of his pistol.

Paralyzed, Tony stood there stupidly while Paul pulled the trigger.

FOR A MOMENT, TONY thought he must be dead. Then Paul swore mildly, and he saw that the towel had jammed the trigger guard. Paul had to take both hands off the trigger for a moment to work it loose.

And in that instant, seizing at his last chance for life, Tony charged in, came in with more speed than seemed possible to generate from his battered frame. Paul danced back, the towel flying loose as he did so. In the confusion, his shot went wide, buried itself in the corner of the room with a rending crash.

With an awkward, twisting lunge, Tony got his left hand on Paul's wrist, chopped at it with his right. The gun roared again, its flash searing his palm, and a knee was jammed cruelly into his groin as Paul closed with him. The world swayed like a hammock.

Then footsteps pounded, and Tony found himself on his hands and knees watching a pair of male figures battering the killer into the wall. His gun clattered to the floor as Lee — a snarling female creature fighting for her (so help her) mate — leaped into the fray and raked her talons across the now groggy killer's face. Then someone landed a terrific right cross, and Paul fell forward on his face, out cold.

"Darling!" gasped Lee, helping Tony to his feet and embracing him shamelessly. "I thought he was going to kill you."

"I knew he was," said Tony.

He looked up, his jaw dropping, into the unattractive features of the broken-nosed man with whom he'd had the fracas early Sunday morning outside of his apartment.

"What in hell are these two doing here?" he snapped, eyeing the intruder's smaller companion, who was sitting on Paul's chest.

"I found them in the hall," she said. "They saved your life."

"I'm sorry," said broken nose, clearing his throat. "We didn't want to get you when you was down, but after the other night, we didn't want to see you till we heard you was banged up in the fight with Maxim."

"Well, thanks for saving me," said Tony, puzzled. "But what in hell do you want?"

"I just want to give you this," said broken nose.

At his signal, his companion calmly lifted Paul's gun, which he'd acquired from the floor, and cracked the butt over Paul's temple. Paul didn't move, didn't look apt to for some time.

Then broken-nose handed Tony a document, and both of them made tracks. Tony blinked, looked at

Lee, shrugged his shoulders. Then he saw the document and sank in a chair.

"Are you okay?" asked Condon, entering then, out of breath.

Tony shook his head.

"I was," he said, "though only just, till I got this."

It was a summons informing him that Maebelle was suing him for divorce. Lee took it from his nervous fingers, examined it closely as Stanton was carried out by a pair of policemen.

"Don't worry," she said, running her fingers through his hair as she perched on the arm of his chair. "Maebelle won't make us any trouble."

"You don't know Maebelle," groaned Tony. "If I pull Phalanx through, I'll be making money, but I won't see any of it."

"No," said Lee triumphantly, "but I will."

"Huh?"

"Maebelle is in a teeny weeny bit of a spot," said Lee, grinning like a Cheshire cat. "She was very careless with some letters. You can prove she was carrying on with at least two other men. And one of them has *mooooney!*"

"But I haven't got the letters," said Tony.

"No," said Lee, "but I have."

"How'd *you* ever get them, honey?" Tony began to show interest.

"Remember last night when Lieutenant Condon made me search the women?" she said. "Well, I had to go through their bags."

"Lee! You didn't!" he said.

"If I didn't, I don't know what I put in my bureau drawer when I came home. Tomorrow we can go right downtown and file a counterclaim — unless, of course, Maebelle listens to reason. And they're really beyootiful letters."

"For Pete's sake!" said Condon, turning on them now that Paul was safely carted away. "Will somebody tell me what happened?"

Tony did, and the lieutenant shook his head.

"Seems to me," he said thoughtfully, "that you've been pushed around by everybody."

"I guess I'm out of condition," he said, looking down at himself. Then, "Lee, what in hell did you do with my clothes?"

"Sent them out to be pressed," she said. "They needed it."

"Honey, I give up. But how come you told Paul where I was?"

"I was dumb," she said frankly. "So dumb I nearly lost you. Poor lamb! Paul called and said he had to see you. I said he couldn't, so he asked if he could send you a wire, and I told him where you were, like a dope. He's a persuasive devil."

"He'll need more than persuasiveness," said Condon later, after Paul had talked. "I can take over from there. She called me about twenty minutes later. She was beginning to wonder if she hadn't made a mistake. And by then I had Paul pretty well cased as our man. I told her so, and she got here a bit ahead of me. Your two process server pals were the Johnnies-on-the-spot though."

"You're telling me," said Tony. Then he laughed. "The other night, when he went for his summons, I thought he was going for a gun. I must have scared him and his pal to death."

"I'm glad you didn't quite," said Condon. "But for them it might have been another ghastly boner like the Pierce business on my part. And by the way, Tony, now we have the killer, I've known you faked that Lamar suicide from the first. Your fingerprints were all over the place. And as soon as I found Pierce had been there, I knew why."

"What else do you know?" Tony asked. "Come clean, Phil. And why in hell have you been dragging me around on the inside?"

"I thing I've got it pretty well doped out," said Condon, lighting a cigarette. "As for dragging you around, first I half suspected you, then things kept happening to you. I thought I'd better keep you under foot."

"That's not news now," said Tony. "I'm half dead from those 'things' that kept happening to me."

Lee gave him a sympathetic smile, turned his face up and kissed him. Condon ignored them blandly until she'd finished.

"Well, here it is," he said quietly. "Paul started it, of course. He wasn't figuring on murder at first, but he wanted Pierce out of the way. He figured it meant a lot of money to him to get Phalanx going as he wanted it."

"How did *you* learn that?" Tony asked.

Condon made a deprecating gesture.

"You fellows aren't the only ones who can read income tax reports," he said. "Anyway, the obvious weak spot in Pierce's armor was the old Lamar scandal. And fate played into his hands, first, when his girl, Connie Talbot, told him about the agoraphobe in the Van Dyke; secondly, when Hy Maxim, a born blackmailer, was shrewd enough to scent out the true situation in Phalanx and approach Paul with the real dope on Lamar and Janet."

"That, of course, was too much for an opportunist like Paul to let get away," said Tony.

"It was," said Condon. "By the way, it seems that Maxim — who can show even our friend Satterlee a few tricks in shakedown rackets — went to Satterlee and bulldozed him out of the proof that Lamar was still alive. Lamar had once been Satterlee's friend. He felt a kinship with him as a fellow wreck. In fact, it was Satterlee who got him into the Van Dyke."

"I gather dear Leon finally talked," said Lee.

"That's right," said the lieutenant. "He made a statement to the sanitarium attendants as soon as they told him Maxim was safely behind bars.

"At any rate, the setup was perfect for Paul. He used Maxim as his stooge to contact young Rideout.

As he hoped, Rideout took it directly to Pierce. Pierce was terrified of the scandal and stalled. So, to Paul's amazement, Rideout put the whole mess back in his lap and told him to hop to it.

"I don't think he liked this setup. It meant that his and Maxim's presence behind the scenes might be exposed, thus laying bare the whole plot to discredit Pierce. And he liked it even less when Pierce finally took action and made steps toward a reconciliation — I guess he had a belated attack of parental love and overcame his fear of the skeleton in his closet."

"That," said Tony, "*would* jam his plans up."

"It did. Satterlee was bound to come up, and then Maxim would be in the soup. And he didn't kid himself that Maxim would hesitate to squeal. So he conceived his scheme for eliminating Lamar and framing Pierce with the murder. He lifted Pierce's gun and wallet in Philadelphia last Friday night.

"Then he arranged to have Connie Talbot get the girl out of the way with her publicity story, went up in the old freight elevator — it could only stop at the seventh floor, remember — walked down a flight and did it. He must have taken a towel from Connie's room to keep it quiet.

"Satterlee nearly caught him, but he got away up the stairs, towel and all, before he was recognized. Then, when he got to Philadelphia, he read, to his surprise and horror, that it was a suicide. He came back to town in a hurry, and Connie called him. We have records of all the Van Dyke calls from the switchboard.

"She was sore — but plenty. She knew he was tired of her and had been making a play for the girl — Janet had told her about it when they talked. And she called him after her talk with you. She'd found the towel he'd used to deaden the shot, had figured most of it out. So she told him that if he'd stick by her, she'd play ball, but that if he didn't she'd blow the thing wide open.

"That's why she asked you up, Tony. If Paul didn't show, she was going to tell you. Paul had a date with Janet, as you know — he got her out by informing her he could help her find her father's murderer. He wanted to keep on the right side of her because of her connection with young Rideout. She didn't know Malin Pierce was her father then.

"So she went. Aleardy doubting the wisdom of putting up with Connie, whom she barely knew, she'd made up her mind to stay at a hotel. Then she saw Satterlee because he'd promised to help her on account of his friendship with Lamar, and also promised to tell her who her real father was. She was desperate, poor kid.

"Tony, when you and Lee ran into them — Paul and Janet — he faked drunkenness as an alibi for what he had to do. You must have walked into Connie's front door about the time he entered her bedroom. He had a key for that.

"He listened in on you, waited until she came in to get the towel — and let her have it. Meanwhile, Satterlee, who had returned from his talk with Janet, found his files torn up. Maxim had taken care of that. He didn't like poor Connie and snooped around the upper stairways where he'd seen the murderer leaving Lamar's apartment.

"Once more he saw his killer, and once again, thanks to the dim hall light and his poor eyesight, he failed to recognize him. But he spotted the towel Paul was taking with him."

"So that's where you got the towel business!" said Tony.

"I want a drink," said Condon. "My throat is drying up."

Lee got him one, which he sipped copiously.

"Meanwhile," he said, talking slowly, "Maxim had been prowling around on the fringe of things on his own, trying to develop a few new angles for shakedowns — and that got him into a peck of trouble.

"He forged M. P.'s name to a note and went to see you. He knew from Paul's letter you were going to figure in the big game and wanted a look at you. So he ran smack into me, which he didn't like at all, but brazened it out. Incidentally, I'm afraid he's going to live. And we haven't got enough on him to put him away for a tenth of what he has coming to him."

"It's my guess he's had quite a bellyful already," said Tony, smiling wryly. "Man! He can handle his dukes. He's the toughest apple I ever fought." He felt the side of his face tenderly.

"You know the rest," said Condon. "You ought to. When your man Martin located Maxim this morning and we got the key to that safety deposit box, we really had the case solved. There was, of course, the matter of Malin Pierce's murder. And that, if it had stood alone, would have been to damn close to being a perfect crime for comfort.

"Paul knew he had to do it as soon as he heard Pierce was on his way up to Rideout's apartment. When Janet Lamar left her handkerchief in her chair, he picked it up — that was when we were all watching the detective who announced Satterlee's arrival. He was reaching for red herrings, and that was a pip.

"When Satterlee headed for the lavatory, he transferred his unpleasant attentions to him. He waited until Leon was about ready to come out, deliberately bumped into him and smashed his glasses.

"He went through the lavatory himself, locked the door, and crawled out the window onto the terrace. When he'd shot Pierce, he came back through the window — he's a wiry, agile cuss — and returned to the party. He'd used the handkerchief to eliminate any chance of leaving his fingerprints on the gun handle. He'd smashed Satterlee's specs, of course, so he wouldn't be recognized.

"And there you have it, Tony, you rat. If you hadn't mucked the whole thing up at the beginning, Pierce, much as I hate to admit it, would have been meat for the electric chair and brother Paul might well have gotten away with it — unless Maxim forced his hand. And with that much money at stake, Maxim would have kept his trap closed, especially as he was implicated himself."

"Well, Pierce was killed anyway, so he wouldn't have lost much either way," said Lee matter-of-factly.

Condon winced at her unmorality, finished his drink and got up.

"So long, kids," he said, "and congratulations all around. Tony, from what I've seen of this girl of yours, you'd better be good to her or else."

"You're not kidding," laughed Tony.

Condon waved farewell from the door and left. Tony heaved a sigh of relief, then sat up sharply.

"Honey," he said. "What about my clothes?"

"Darling," said Lee. "You aren't leaving for a while. Now that we've got Maebelle's claws pulled —"

"I've got to go," he said, "much as I love you."

"Where are you going?" she asked suspiciously.

"Philadelphia," he told her quietly. "There's work to be done — and I mean work."

"Tony!" she wailed. "You can't leave me up here alone."

"*Can't* I," he said. "I'm doing it. You're too valuable in Manhattan right now. Carl won't be able to talk intelligibly until he gets his teeth in, and I can't find a substitute for both of us — until tomorrow, anyway."

He grinned at her open anger.

"I'll meet you at Broad Street Station at seven o'clock tonight," he concluded. "And sign out of this dump. We'll be making new arrangements."

"Tony, you beast!" she cried, and flung herself into his lap. He yipped.

"God!" he yelled. "My ribs!"

But he didn't really mind the pain in his ribs.

THE END